# BOULDER

# *Boulder*

EVA BALTASAR

*translated by Julia Sanches*

London · New York · Sydney · Toronto · New Delhi

PARAMOUNT

This edition published in India by Simon & Schuster India, 2023

Simon & Schuster India
818, Indraprakash Building,
21, Barakhamba Road,
New Delhi 110001.

Originally published as *Boulder* by Club Editor in 2020
First edition in English, 2022, And Other Stories



1 3 5 7 9 8 6 4 2

ISBN: 978-93-92099-69-4
eBook ISBN: 978-93-92099-70-0

This book has been selected to receive financial assistance from English PEN's PEN Translates programme, supported by Arts Council England. English PEN exists to promote literature and our understanding of it, to uphold writers' freedoms around the world, to campaign against the persecution and imprisonment of writers for stating their views, and to promote the friendly co-operation of writers and the free exchange of ideas. www.englishpen.org

Simon & Schuster India is committed to sourcing paper that is made from wood grown in sustainable forests and support the Forest Stewardship Council, the leading international forest certification organisation.

Our books displaying the FSC logo are printed on FSC certified paper.


Printed and bound in India by Replika Press Pvt. Ltd.

Supported using public funding by
**ARTS COUNCIL ENGLAND**

Love is a solitary thing.

CARSON McCULLERS
*The Ballad of the Sad Café*

# 1

Quellón. Chiloé. A night years ago. Sometime after ten. No sky, no vegetation, no ocean. Only the wind, the hand that grabs at everything. There must be a dozen of us. A dozen souls. In a place like this, at a time like now, you can call a person a soul. The wharf is small and sloped. The island surrenders to the water in concrete blocks with a number of cleats bolted to them in a row. They look like the deformed heads of the colossal nails that pin the dock to the seabed. That's all. I'm amazed at the islanders' stillness. They sit scattered under the rain beside large objects the size of trunks. Swaddled in windproof plastic, they eat in silence with thermoses locked between their thighs. They wait. The rain pounds down as though cursing at them, runs along their hunched backs and forms rivulets that flow into the sea, the enormous mouth that never tires of swallowing, receiving. The cold feels peculiar. It's possible I've drunk some of it myself, since I can feel it thrashing and bucking under my skin, and also deeper inside, in the arches between each organ. Impenetrable islanders. I've been here for three months, working as a cook at a couple of summer camps for teenagers. In the evenings I would cycle to town and drink aguardiente at the hostel bar. There were barely any women.

It was a workers' ritual. Stained teeth bared in greeting. The jet-black eyes of every family tree that's managed to grow on this salty rock speak to me from their tables. They speak to me for all of the dead.

I'm not a chef, I'm just a mess-hall cook, capable and self-taught. The thing I most enjoy about my job is handling food while it's still whole, when some part of it still speaks of its place in the world, its point of origin, the zone of exclusion that all creatures need in order to thrive. Water, earth, lungs. The perfect conditions for silence. Food comes to us wrapped in skin, and to prepare it you need a knife. If I've got one skill in the kitchen, it's carving things up. The rest is hardly an art. Seasoning, tossing things together, applying heat . . . Your hands end up doing it all on their own. I've worked at schools, nursing homes, in a prison. Each job only lasts a few weeks, they slip away from me, spots of grease that I gradually scrub off. The last boss I had before coming to Chiloé tried to give me an explanation: the problem isn't the food, it's you. Kitchens require team effort. I'd have to find a really small one if I wanted to work on my own and still make a living.

The ship arrives at midnight. It barrels toward us at an alarming speed. Or at least that's how it looks, because of the light glaring in the downpour, making us blink. There's movement behind us too; someone's pulled up in a jeep and left the engine running. He calls us. The islanders rise. They look like enormous turtles hatched from a large egg. They plod through the rain, and as they pass me I feel like an insignificant foreigner, disease-white and sopping wet under my dark blue rain jacket. You'd need two of me to make one body as tough as theirs. But I was like them once, despite everything. I'd dug into the island with my nails and learned that the pulp of your fingers can harden, that the heart governs the body and shapes it according to its highest mandate: the will. We huddle around the driver's door. I use my hood as a visor, rub my eyes, and try to make sense of what's happening. Hands exchange coins, bills. From the car radio comes the sound of string music, as though in honor of the storm. I buy a ticket with pesos from my belt bag. The rest of my three months' salary is wrapped in plastic, tucked between my undershirt and my skin.

It's as if the sea itself has held out the gangway, as if the ocean has come to collect us. My backpack has me walking at an angle. I've got ropes in each fist and I let them lead the way. The yelling keeps us moving. As I board the ship I think it's not actually that big, and then—silence. Human sounds are virtually imperceptible, here, beyond the reach of the elements. We walk sideways, with cautious steps, down a metal staircase. Behind a door is an empty hold. This is a freighter, not a cruise ship. We let ourselves fall inside as though we'd been adrift for years, and some of us exchange looks, possibly for the first time. The man next to me pulls out a bottle of pisco and takes a long swig. Then he passes it around. A pipe ceremony: we'll see how it ends. I shrug off the rain jacket and my drenched sweater, then throw on a dry, dirty one I find after rooting blindly through my pack. I don't know when we set sail. The hold rises and falls nonstop. Now and then we all slide to one side and the light bulb flickers until the sea surges again, sending us back to where we were before. An old woman passes me the bottle with a smile in each eye and a toothless grin. I take it and drink. I love this place, these narrow black eyes that neither desire me nor reject me, this fabulous freedom.

It's what I came here looking for, true zero. I was tired of inventing résumés, of having to pretend life had a structure, as though there were a metal rod inside me keeping me upright and steady. The destination always kills the journey, and if we have to reduce life to a story, it can only be a bad one. What was I thinking, dropping everything for a three-month contract on the other side of the world? I'd just been fired from a restaurant in an industrial park. I used to hitchhike there every morning. Most of the time I was late, even though I gave myself two hours to make the trip. The best part of my day was when a car or van stopped on the side of the road, a hundred and fifty meters or so ahead, and summoned me with its blinkers. I'd run toward it like a lunatic, backpack on and jacket open, blowing out clouds of breath and cigarette smoke into the cold air. Some drivers were surprised when they saw I was a woman. Others didn't even notice. Fifteen kilometers of peace, of being nowhere, of intruding on the commutes of kind people who had to suffer through them every single day. I often wished I could've jumped out of those cars while they were still moving, instead of having to say a polite goodbye and close their doors the way you might close the casket of a good friend, an inanimate body. What was I thinking, dropping everything? The devastating possibility of the same old job, of a tiny room in a suburban apartment, of lovers as fleeting as shooting stars, hot to the touch one day, a distant dream the next. The days came and went, unchanging, and every night I tossed them back one swig at a time, stretched out on my narrow bed with headphones in my ears and an ashtray on my chest. I'd gone through life fixated on an intangible conviction, tied down by the handful of things that kept me from becoming penniless, an outcast. I needed to face the emptiness, an emptiness I had dreamed of so often I'd turned it into a mast, a center of gravity to hold onto when life fell to pieces around me. I'd come from nothing, polluted, and yearned for windswept lands.

A hard floor and a bag for a pillow. Quiet companions. Me inside the hold, the hold inside the storm, an envelope of cash next to my stomach. This night I've won.

. . .

I stick around for a few years. The captain has a gambler's face, patient and smart. They call him *patrón*. His skin is fine and red and rises out of his shirt collar like a second shirt clinging to his tiny features: chin, mouth, mustache, nose, forehead, all in a line, one after the other, with two hole-like eyes that drive home his every decision and order. He offered me the job because I didn't ask for money, just room and board. I think I've discovered what happiness is: whistling the moment you wake up, not getting in anyone's way, owing no explanations, and falling into bed at daybreak, body addled from exhaustion and mind free of every last trace of bitterness and dust. Everyone on board thinks I'm certifiable, that I'm the black sheep of an aristocratic family, that someone murdered my parents and siblings and I'm here lying low with an anonymous crew so that I can plan out every detail of a slow, cold-blooded revenge. I let them believe it because they're friendly and because at the end of the day we're more like family than if we'd shared the same mother. We all incubate here in the boat's amniotic fluid; the boat loves and nurtures us, it invites us to take another look at ourselves. I let myself be strung along; life develops without overwhelming me, it squeezes into every minute, it implodes; I hold it in my hands. I can give anything up, because nothing is essential when you refuse to imprison life in a narrative.

We sail back up the coast of Chile. All the way to Talcahuano, Valparaíso, Antofagasta, Iquique. I don't usually disembark, even though now and then I get the urge—in Valparaíso, for example, a night port under the cover of gleaming *cerros*. I want to keep a lover there. I sit on deck, drink, smoke half a pack of cigarettes, and feel stupid. It's been over a year since I held a woman in my arms. My body rails at me, it demands another body to touch and stimulate and use to satisfy its own monstrous hunger—until that person, her purity, her charms are used up and spat out. I'm dying to open and close a door, to pull another mouth to bed with my mouth, to parcel out desire. It was easy in Barcelona. Here, I don't even bother. Better to just retreat to my bunk and recall everything to that concrete point between my legs while the saliva on my fingers fills me with tobacco and solitude.

This is the best job I've ever had. The galley is small and rusted. One oven, four burners, a countertop. The pots look like they were salvaged from the bottom of the sea. It's a good thing I brought my own knives. I don't even take my eyes off them at night. If I left them in a drawer, the next day I'd have to fetch them from the engine room. Still, no one steps foot in the galley when I'm there. The door stays open, and every now and then someone pokes their head in to ask for coffee. They can brew it themselves. I've got water on the boil around the clock, a jar of instant coffee and another of white sugar. Sometimes they sit on the stool in the corner. They relax and watch me work and tell me about their grandmothers—all experts in the kitchen, all queens of humitas and empanadas. The second mate reads out the recipe to me. Humitas are out of the question, but I develop an interest in empanadas. They're practical and everyone likes them, even though the meat I use is tinned and the olives need more brine. I start the dough in the evenings and let it rise all night. I like to get under the covers knowing that out there another covered body lies awake, working on my behalf. In the morning I'm amazed by how much it's risen, as if the whole thing—the soft, perfect dome of wheat and its nest-bowl of warmth—were a distant nephew who's grown up, effortlessly and all of a sudden, in the silence of my absence. I knead the bread, dust it with flour, shape it and take its shape, and imagine I am a simpleminded god about to beget a new tribe. Anything not to feel the hips, the ass, the breasts, the perfect flesh of a woman beneath my hands.

We spend whole weeks in the Sea of Chiloé. It's an uncomfortable body of water, like it doesn't feel at home caught between the continent and the archipelago. The worst storms, no comparison to my first time on board. The waters get so rough we have to seek shelter in a bay. Hours of waiting, most often at night. If we're carrying passengers, I have someone take down some sandwiches for them. The locals are thrilled. Each bite seems to enrich and fortify them, to give them more life and the strength to live it. The few tourists on board, on the other hand, are disappointed in everything. Strange, given that they'd made a point of shunning the comforts of ocean liners. They'd left home ready to turn their holiday into an expedition, a quest for some kind of inner truth. After researching freighters with room for passengers, they'd bought tickets on a stormy night, feeling more alive than ever and loving their sense of adventure more than they loved the children they already had or might go on to have. Three hours in and they're livid; they need the bathroom. Theirs is on deck. Two staircases up from the hold, then another to the annex. The wind spits in their faces, blinding them with pellets from this austral downpour. The waves roar, they'd swallow everything if they could. I don't understand how these people manage to keep alive. They pant violently and cling to nonexistent handrails as they make their way up. They empty themselves in the toilet. The waves are in there too, like a sea monster that surges up and slams them to the wall, then consumes them neck-first. If I ever turn out like them, I swear to God I'll shoot myself.

I'm not sure why I start earning a salary. Nothing out of this world, except it changes my relationship with work, which doesn't feel like it's mine anymore but instead belongs to someone who values it and deigns to give it to me. I feel a sense of loss, though I'd been in the red for a while and needed the money. I still make the best food I can, my new owner's invisible leash slack but present. In Chaitén, I stock up on tobacco, tampons, deodorant, and socks. Funny how socks go missing. I buy red ones so I'll know which ones are mine. Chaitén is a regular stop and I almost always disembark, if only for a couple of hours. The streets are long and empty, as wide as airstrips. A full-bodied woman serves coffee and cake in the dining room of her small house. The best lemon cake in the world. It's always packed in there, despite the floral drapes, the ornate dinnerware, and the rugs. She also has rooms available. Whenever we dock for more than twenty-four hours, I reserve one so that I can have a hot shower and sleep in a real bed with a wooden frame that can support my every thought and moan. On days when it rains, I feel like I've just come home after conquering the world. That's where I met Samsa and where, for a few moments, I became conscious of the magma seething beneath the miracle of our oceans and continents.

Five in the evening. It's already dark out. I order coffee, drop my bag on the floor, and make my way to one of the few seats available, next to a pair of townies and a boy busy dunking his fingers in the tea. She's at a table in the back with five or six other people. White-blonde hair, swimmer's shoulders. There are corporate logos on their knapsacks and jackets, which hang from their chairs. They speak in hushed voices, like Scandinavians abroad, or like people who've just struck oil. I can't not look at her, like when you peer over the edge of a boat and come face-to-face with a shark. I forget to add sugar to my coffee, I burn my tongue. I feel the hardness of the rock in which desire has become lodged, as if for all time. I look at her and feel woozy, even though she's Scandinavian and makes her living from a multinational with blood on its hands. I look at her and she fills every corner of me. My gaze is a rope that catches her and draws her in. She looks up, sees me. She knows.

We spend the night together. I don't fuck her, I whet myself on her. I drink her like I'd been raised wandering the desert. I swallow her as if she were a sword, little by little and with enormous care. The hours layer over one another, blanketing us. I wake up at half past five with just enough time to make it back to the ship. I don't know how to leave her, it's like the waxy parts of my body have hardened to her shape. I kiss her and kiss her. I kiss the hair that falls over her eyes and casts them in a weird golden light. I kiss her tensed neck and her exquisite back, her nipples flat and unfeeling after so many hours of night. I close her eyes and kiss their blue color by kissing the skin it shows through. I suck on her unfamiliar, exhausted tongue. My kisses are landmines. I set them mindlessly, easy as humming, knowing that when I come back they'll explode, dismember, unearth bodies and quarries. We exchange numbers. I cling to her the way lunatics embrace new beliefs or dangle from trees. I leave. We'll see each other in less than three moons. Three moons. Those are the words that leave my mouth.

I think about her all the time. My body is like a lab where a circle of alchemists is working on developing the ultimate rock, her light one of a million possibilities that I am obsessed by. It takes every bit of focus I have to make food. I buy a Greek cookbook from a secondhand bookstore in Puerto Montt. Spices, fresh vegetables, cheese, lamb. Tiny anchors that fasten my mind to solid ground. I cook with the door closed, like I'm a genius for whose work the audience must learn to wait with patience. The truth is I'm intoxicated. Samsa courses through my veins. My fingers enter her as I gut the lamb. Three months, in which we steer into Peruvian waters. We sail farther than ever before, and it feels like we're on the run. Not a single phone call or text message. Nothing. Hummus, moussaka, and a very challenging baklava recipe sprinkled with pisco and honey. The captain sings my praises. I don't know what else to do with my hands.

We start seeing each other. I call her before we dock in Chaitén, and she jumps into her pickup truck and drives the eight hours there. We meet at the inn. She rolls up, parks, switches off the engine. My body is nervy as I open the door and dump all of her toxins onto the immaculate bed inside me. I've never felt so merciless, so inhuman. I kiss her as if I could dissolve the skin of desire that coats her lips and teeth. We shut ourselves in the room. Sometimes we can meet up every ten days, sometimes after a month or two. I've ordered a strapless strap-on that arrives by airmail from the United States. I pick it up from a P.O. box in Ancud. It's beautiful, the electric-blue color of the water where wrasses live among corals. Fucking her with a strap-on is like waking up summer and drowning it in its own swelter, it's tossing her way up high and fighting the undertow that pulls me under before I give in to the quiet. For hours and hours. Time drips off our bodies, trickles between our legs, we tack it to the walls. I kiss her like I never knew I could kiss anyone, giving her everything I've held back for her while we're apart, when she's not with me.

She doesn't like my name, and gives me a new one. She says I'm like those large, solitary rocks in southern Patagonia, pieces of world left over after creation, isolated and exposed to every element. No one knows where they came from. Not even they understand how they're still standing and why they never break down. I tell her I've seen rocks like those in the middle of the ocean. The ships skirt them in silence, as though some mythological creature could awaken and attack them. They're not always by themselves. Sometimes there are more just a short distance away. Sometimes they form labyrinths you would be wise to avoid. Samsa lets her hair down and tickles my forehead, my eyelashes, my neck. She calls me Boulder and I don't know why we laugh. Maybe love is unfurling above us like an enormous branch that bends and touches all the most sensitive, reticent parts of us.

I have never felt so strange on board. I've lost something that used to belong to me alone—to me and this ship. We sail and everything feels the same. The coast of Chile is black, and it shrouds every last hint of humanity in a way that's almost romantic, moving. Wooden piers whose piles are constantly soaking, like the swollen legs of someone with gout. Crevices where life is a teeming kingdom of mollusks. The dark oxide that the ocean breathes out and that crawls upland like fungus—the simplest, most expansive creature on earth. My breath catches when we drop anchor. I feel like I'm following it down into an ocean-deep silence where everything dies. The galley is too small, my bunk bed's a joke, the few common spaces on board are unbearable. In the evenings I sit on deck and look out at the lights of the houses in the distance. Now and then one of them quivers as if struck by a rod. I smoke more than ever, but smoking alone at night is just another way to heighten the magic, to conjure up the desired body and coax it in little by little—until it's reached my oxygen reserves, until it's made it to my most tender memories, trapped in the solid box of my chest.

I've done a lot of thinking. A Uruguayan therapist said on the radio that travel promotes mental activity; in other words, living on a ship is about as good as it gets. I think in order to plaster over my feelings. I picture my thoughts as a herd of buffalo or zebu crossing the predator-infested waters of my peace of mind, of everything I've managed to build up on this ship, one plate at a time. I can't stand herds, that mad and singular desire, that vastness in their gaze—almost panicked, virtually sacrificial. I try to steer clear of them. I don't study myself; I think. Actually, I take myself apart.

Thinking loosens me up, as if I were a longbow. I learn to play chess from a sailor with something of an obsession. He always beats me, though it takes him longer every day. I also pick up a couple of mindless hobbies that demand my full attention, like French patisserie and distilling quinces into brandy. I have a lot of fun getting the crew drunk and fat. I don't even notice life carrying me away. I've found the perfect wave and I ride it as if I'd tamed it, as if everything hinged on the luck that I hand out, driven by the appetites of generosity.

Months pass, perfect and luminous, then one day she tells me she's leaving. She says it with tears in her eyes, trembling and hesitant like a kid who doesn't want to jump in the water. We're sitting in bed, facing each other. It's midafternoon and looks like rain, it could've been a phenomenal night. I gaze down at her hands. She's fiddling with one of my rings. They don't fit her, though now and then she likes to slip them down to her knuckles and make fun of me. She says things that are dirtier than anything I've heard on board and digs them into my skin. I stop her with my hand and stroke her belly in a steady motion, like the critical moment in a concert when the conductor invites the other instruments to join. I wipe her tears with my thumbs. I look down at my chest, smooth and bare except for a fresh bitemark and a tattoo of Chiloé. How can this intense locus of pain not be bleeding? She's accepted a position in Reykjavík. A good opportunity, she says. The room spins as if on stilts, the dramatic scene inside making it dance. I love her. I can think of only one person I'd kill for her. She looks at me without asking and I nod. Then I hold her like I want to get her drunk and make her forget love and all the coins in her newfound treasure. Rain begins to fall. Life tears open like a wound that rots and bubbles. If anyone talks to me about happiness, I swear to God I'll break their face.

# 2

Reykjavík. We live in a small apartment across from the harbor. Samsa works more than ten hours a day, even though she only has one job—everyone else here has two. She makes a lot of money. Life in this city is expensive, but our checking account balance resembles the generational wealth of a cheap, unwedded aunt. Samsa thinks we should buy a place. I tell her I'm not interested, that I haven't come all this way to play house. I'll keep the apartment. A single thirty-square-meter space. A kitchen-cum-dining room with a bed in the back, lonely as a rowboat. The glass walls take in the whole bay, from end to end. The sea around Iceland is a dreadful thing, and I wouldn't have enjoyed sailing on it. Misty and cold, always the same shade of smoky blue. But I like having it there, in front of our bed. When Samsa straddles me, breasts thrust up at the night like coastlines, the candlelight casts her reflection on the water and I feel like I'm a galleon on the verge of shipwreck, like she is my figurehead.

It isn't long before I start looking for work. Samsa says I don't have to, that I can stay home and do my own thing, or else explore the area. She tells me to take some time off and settle into the new place. *Do my own thing. Time off.* Language is and always will be an occupied territory. I have the feeling I was shackled to it the moment I was born. Only language can help you belong somewhere and make sure you don't lose your way. It's a nourishing underlayer that seems to live in the mind, migrate down to the mouth, and, spoken, melt on the lips. At the same time, language is everywhere, occupying the body's farthest-flung cells, pushing them to unimaginable places. It urges you on and turns your stomach, confuses your animal instincts, makes you human. No emotion is more indulgent than feeling that you are intensely human. Though it can also be the most tyrannical. You are responsible for every word, and no statement is innocent. Sometimes, Samsa's make me wonder if I've made a mistake loving her with such ease. But it means everything to hold her in my arms, her body steadfast to mine, happiness flowing from her limbs like the vigorous power of a god, knowing without a doubt that this is my all. That I can believe in her firmly—even from a distance, a hood over my head.

She bought it. A little yellow house surrounded by other pretty little houses on the outskirts of the city. Two stories, basement, backyard, enough bedrooms to put up an entire nation. The kind of living quarters that give me the chills. Sometimes I have the feeling they all come equipped with a full retinue of ghosts itching to haunt you into an early grave.

So much for Canterville. These new, single-family homes have ravenous souls that feed off of your own little human soul—sucking dry your freedom, your independence, and all trace of your passion. You shut yourself in every night and bolt the door, convinced it's safer that way, when in reality you're betraying yourself: you pull up the blanket and rest your head on the pillow, offering up your jugular. The house gathers itself up and looms over you. It unhinges its jaw like those terrifying snakes that bleed the milk from sleeping mothers then curl up like necklaces against their skin. Samsa leases it to a couple with three children. She says the kitchen is so beautiful that I'd want to roll out a mattress on the floor and never leave if I ever saw it. Sometimes I think she doesn't quite get me. Quaint little houses like hers eat away at you. Bit by bit. They bore deep into you and strike the most delicate nerve. By the time you notice, it's too late. You've already been killed by the kind of devastating energy that can only come from pain.

I don't like them, Icelanders. They feel so insular, tribal. I envy their strength, their asymptomatic bodies, the painful brightness of their eyes. They're born with pieces of their enormous island inside them, as they grow old they become attached to them and as adults they emanate an almost earthly force that seems to celebrate them and bring them closer together. I can put up with them one-on-one, but in groups I find them exhausting. Samsa is really sociable and has made plenty of friends. Which is unsurprising. She has this ethereal gift for drawing to her own light the less gentle and less captivating light of other people, who then have the urge to touch her and feel as though they shine brighter. There isn't a week that goes by when we don't have to socialize. With friends she's made at work, yoga, the gym, the Spanish lessons she enrolled in so she could have something of mine, she said, as though by loaning each other our languages we were giving sustenance to one another. If I charged for every meal I cook on weekends, I'd make a tidy living. The worst thing about these get-togethers, though, isn't the get-together itself—following the thread of the conversation, laughing at the right moment, nodding like a strange species of bird that's been set loose in an aviary full of wilder and more beautiful birds. No. The worst thing is the children. Icelanders are slaves to biology, breeders. They begin to have children when they're still in their teens—countless cubs, feral and blond like their Viking ancestors. They form extensive clans and take their kids with them wherever they go, like marsupials. The whole country is set up for it. I'm not into kids. I find them annoying. They're unpredictable variables that come crashing into my coastal shelf with the gale force of their natural madness. They're craggy, out of control, scattered. They're drawn to me the same way cats zero in on people who are allergic to them. Samsa welcomes these kids with cookies, their parents forget about them, and I make sure everyone stays lubricated. Glasses, bottles, ice. They're walls behind which I shelter, as if those extremely high-proof green and lilac liquors could keep them all on the far side of my world. I don't know why it doesn't work. Halfway through the meal the kids start climbing on me, getting their partly chewed food all over my jeans and begging me to pay attention to them, fuss over them, talk to them. The more I ignore them, the more they insist. Samsa looks at me and smiles. The fact that she's moved, the fact that she thinks of me as a challenge and believes she can train me the way a farmer would train a wolf—it drives me up the fucking wall.

I find work at a Chinese restaurant and a local pub. It's like I've regressed. I spend half the day washing dishes at the Chinese place and nights preparing unpronounceable appetizers in a hovel where I'd love to find some dark corner to get drunk in with Samsa on my lap. Despite the hours, the low wages, and the repetitive work, I feel good. My bosses at the Chinese restaurant don't take notice of me. To them I'm just a fellow work-denizen, a machine that sucks up stuff that's dirty and makes it clean and dry in a set amount of time. The demanding rhythm isolates me from my colleagues, myself, my past and all my deep-seated memories. From everything. There are only two of us in the pub kitchen, me and the boss. All I have to do is follow orders, there's no need to coordinate. He instructs and I execute. Under my domain are the shellfish, the cod, and the shark. I work the supplies without gloves on, my skin to their flesh. The knife glides like a pencil that can cut through paper. There are moments when I feel almost sacred, as if the counter were an altar. If doing my own thing had to mean something, it would be this: battening down at work like an oyster in a shell, serving as the hand that makes a pearl out of a foreign body—for no reason at all, except that maybe there's a pulp of meaning to this solitude capable of revealing the solitude of every tiny creature in a species, of a single ecosystem throughout time. Exhaustion is a spirit that only manifests in the dead of night, when the kitchen is so packed we have to work with the doors wide open. Before heading home, I scrub the burner and the floor and have a glass of brennivín with the servers. Or two. Or three. It's nothing like pisco. Sweet and aromatic in comparison, and so strong it makes my whole day melt away, as if all those hours of work were a tumor that had been growing inside me since morning, minute by minute, until finally it occupies me completely and forces me into exile. Alcohol is the storm that makes clarity collapse and waste away.

We spend holidays in bed and, if I close my eyes, we're back in Chaitén. I feel stronger with Samsa's body underneath mine, like she is my foundation. I fuck her with a thirst that seems to contain more than just the need for sex. I rush, I inhibit her. I strip her clothes with my teeth and follow her scent with flared nostrils, ruthless, as if wanting to unearth a treasure. Desire overwhelms me, in the way I hold her and withhold from her a desire that is identical, jealous, borderline cruel. I cling to her until she has swallowed my fingers and allowed my hand to follow and make a fist like a mad heart. Love runs down my arms and slaps her. If I stop, she shakes. If I lose her, she swears. Satisfying her is like settling a blood debt. We fall back exhausted; a sense of peace grows around me, as predictable as a ripple in water.

We travel around the country. For a geologist like Samsa, Iceland is paradise, and she shows me around as if it had come out of her own body. I like them, these outings. Flat, empty highways, the landscape blanketed always in green, always in lichen, always in blue. Water wanders the land with fetal vigor; it retreats and gathers strength, then shoots, yells, falls. The earth flaunts it. We have a massive car that can get us anywhere. Samsa drives it with a singular passion, knowing where she's going but not what she'll find there. She has a hard time lending the car to me, as though it were an animal loyal to its human and unyielding with everyone else. We make our way inland following paths invisible to the human eye. She calls them veins and promises they're stable. I don't know whether she's joking or she's lying. I haven't been able to figure out when she's going to stop, or why. We park in the middle of nowhere, she tells me to get out, we tool up and start walking. For hours. It's important to wear waterproof clothes, and to bring a GPS, a cell phone, food. She stops often to collect samples and take photographs. She's educating me, or at least she thinks she is. She talks to me like I'm a dumb colleague—eyes wide open, hands tensed, and mouth slow, enunciating each word. Her kingdom is the original kingdom, history in a pure state, a large illustration encased in volcanic rock that she uncovers with language whose precision comes from being learned. I let her walk ahead of me and concentrate on her ass. Moments like this, the things she says, interest me about as much as an informational leaflet.

Five years pass. Samsa has kept moving up at work, like a goat braving the Dolomites' slatelike ridges, climbing straight up to the highest peak. When there's nothing more for her to aspire to, she changes jobs. She works for an oil company. She travels a lot, sometimes for weeks on end. Her suitcase is always in sight, black pants and a black blazer, white shirt and a pair of heels. When she leaves the house dressed like that, at the crack of dawn, I feel like a beloved servant entrusted with a heavy set of keys. She gives me an uncertain kiss—neither short nor long, and completely empty of her—then promptly shuts the door, more powerful than ever. That's when I realize there's a living thing seated inside me; in fact it's lounging around and whistling as it watches the sky slowly descend as if dancing. I'm always surprised by the lack of guilt in that place where love, which always pushes outward, meets solitude, which always pulls inward. My love doesn't leave with Samsa, but it isn't part of me either. It belongs to desire. This is exactly what it means to love her—to want her company with every fiber of cloth and mind, from the marrow of each and every bone. To want it with every army. With hunger, fever, despair. When Samsa leaves, it isn't my love that she takes with her but the love that exists in this house. A powerful love that grows like brambles, strangles the furniture, and girds the walls. A thorny love that watches over me as I fall asleep, its eyes red and always watching, sharp claws sunk into the night.

I switch jobs several times. I still work at the pub now and then, whenever they need an extra body. Which comes in handy if I want to get out of a dinner at the last minute. Samsa doesn't like it when I leave like that, without any warning, even if I set the table and put the salmon to roast in the oven. I tend to wait for her to get in the shower, that way I can blow her a kiss goodbye and quickly shut the door without letting out any steam or having to listen to her complain in a language that isn't mine and never will be. Walking on the dock at night makes me want to join the crew of a boat, an authentic one—rugged, ramshackle, creaky, eaten away by rust; a worn-down muscle. The Icelandic fleet is a thing of beauty. The boats glisten in the dark, polished by the quiet water, which holds them up like an offering. They float side by side, secured to their cleats like obedient animals. When I look at them, they awaken a sluggish pain that makes me hate them before I can admire them—for how modern they are, how well suited to a global ideal embodied in a country that is isolated and yet no less real. It's the same when I look at Samsa, asleep on the still-glowing embers of sex, and hate her the second before I worship her perfection.

. . .

The short term can tether you to the world of senses—the hazardous, inexact border that cuts through the forest. Most of it unchecked. Its greatest virtue is that it keeps you on your toes. At the same time, they removed me from my chosen life. Eight years with Samsa and every millimeter of land has been charted. All of it. How can existence exhaust itself? I contemplate disappearing. I sit on the dock for hours and study my chances of leaving no trace. But I stay put. I wander around and have a cigarette before heading up to the apartment, tired of the heavy, unfeeling boreal light. Smoke rises from my body like morning fog off a large, porous rock. Repetitive thoughts come out of nowhere like rough weather, gathering strength as they cross the ocean, and bursting into my head with such force I'm left feeling like they have it out for me, like they've been trying to track me down so they can whip me to pieces and make me theirs, dead or alive. Loving Samsa has made me cautious. I need an inlet, I need time. That's when I decide to start my own business. I buy a used vehicle. Some acquaintances recommend a service shop and six months later, with all the paperwork in order, I open a food truck.

I feel strange. I'm churned mud, hiding lives that once breathed peacefully and that now startle, pant, and rage. I have no one to blame for the torches and the pitchforks. I don't know what I'm looking for, inside. In fact, I don't know if I'm looking for anything at all. Maybe by attacking myself I'm protecting those close to me from stronger, less noble assaults. Change had burst in like a fledgling beak that pokes around inside me, needlessly harmful. Responsibility isn't particularly heavy and doesn't need to be held; it sutures itself to the brain and contaminates the blood with its narcotic fluids. Blood. Necessary and mortal. The things we pour into it are more nourishing than bodies: the verb that resuscitates it every day, the impulse that moves it, the fire, the spark, the fervor. I can't find my face, so I touch my body and grab at pieces of other bodies that are like mine, except hushed. I wake up every morning, take Samsa some coffee in bed. We say goodbye and I pull on a pair of sneakers. I jog across the city like I'm on the run and come home breathless, doubled over with a stitch in my chest. I cook empanadas and sell them on Parliament Square, from noon to night. I find it hard to believe I make as much money as I do. Before heading home, I stop at the pub. My old boss is called Ragnar and we've become fast friends.

With Ragnar, I've discovered something: other women. The lush, radiant presence of other women. I get to the pub around midnight. Blackened wood, bodies that give off the sweet, wet smell of booze, plates wiped clean. People sit close together, practically on top of one another. They drink and chat, and often raise their voices and argue with broad gestures and pitchers clutched in their hands, as though berating each other. The window catches the light glowing faintly at every table and refracts it into countless fine beams that travel through the space and rise up to the ceiling, weightless as spores. Ragnar and I sit in the very back. It's his table, his worn wooden bench padded with cushions covered in age-old stains. Actually, it's more like a cabin, from which he rules over everything. We drink vodka, brennivín, gin, beer. Bodies drowsy, eyes warm, feet up on the table. He talks to me about people as if I know them all personally. He rates the new servers and raises his glass or cocks the braided end of his beard to greet someone from afar. He says he's been divorced three times, that he's wild about women and would marry again just to be able to bury his hands in a tangle of hair when he falls into bed at night. He talks to me about his ex-wives and his seven or eight kids. All I know is that wife number three had amazing tits. Creamy as skyr, he says. The man's a poet. We smoke in the face of every law, as if somehow our smoke could reveal wonders. The place is packed, even though it's after hours. Ragnar nods toward a woman who's gotten up to go to the bathroom. I realize that any woman, when pointed out to me, becomes *a woman*; she appears to me. It'd been years since a woman had appeared to me. Samsa had banished them all. This woman is tall and has the same powerful complexion as most Icelanders, as if her body held an ever-burning fire in which she forged her courage. I look at her the way I imagine Ragnar does, and it makes me feel flushed, like I need another drink. She pushes through the crowd. Tight jeans, chunky wool sweater. Her hands are shields, pressing into backs and forcing them out of her way. Her body rubs, advancing. My eyes fall on her breasts, the powerful curve of her ass. They seek out her lips. I don't know what's going on with me. Sex has taken control, stiffening certain parts of my body that in turn soften all the others. In my gaze lurks an animal that desires and has no self-control. I drag on my cigarette, exhale. Slow but steady, in and out, as I watch her. If she looks at me she'll know, just like Samsa did. I don't want her to look. At the same time, I'm worse off than Ragnar; I'm horny and feel totally abandoned. Sex—that brutal, rabid urge that conjugal relationships temper and relieve—fizzes like compressed gas out of a crack in the earth. I knock back my drink, get up. I'm going home. A shame, Ragnar says. He's right. I feel at ease here, this may be my favorite place in all of Iceland.

The days have changed too. Like every year, September ends exhausted of light. Icelanders cling to it with a hunger that is vibrant and vulnerable, with a touch of destitution. It's time to fit the houses, to sweep, tidy, and stockpile food. During these weeks, empanadas fly off the shelves so fast it doesn't make sense. I work more than ever, and it's still not enough. Samsa offers to come help one evening. I turn her down. I know she thinks it would be an adventure. I know she loves me. I know we barely see each other. But I need to keep her away from this thing that's all my own—the spice-filled, close-quartered food truck where I cook recipes that made me happy back when all I had was an endless rein too loose to guide my heart, and where nothing at all depended on me.

. . .

And it happens. The thing that has no bearing on my life or on the kilometers-long perimeter of life that was meant to protect me from those permanent, timeless laws, the kind that defy all probability. It comes to the house like a Jonah. Unexpected and unfortunate. A sickness that had only ever affected other people. I want a baby, Samsa says, our baby. Your baby. She says this and I feel nothing, like I've drunk arsenic. All I know is I've gone cold. It's six in the morning. The alarm clock went off half an hour ago so we'd have time to make love. Her idea, her words. She says she never sees me during the day and that we're too tired at night. When she makes sweeping statements like this one, she tends to be talking about herself: when I come home at night, she's asleep and I'm turned on. The goal of having the alarm go off once or twice a week at an ungodly hour is to awaken love. I get up, brush my teeth, and grab the strap-on because it's faster that way. I fuck her and she lets herself be fucked, it looks like she's not even moving. She welcomes in a desire that I'm not giving her and that roams the corridors of her body like a ghost. She holds my chin and makes me look at her while I thrust over and over. I don't enjoy it, I apply myself. She kisses me, as if a kiss could fill the silence that separates two faraway bodies the moment they surrender to each other. She kisses me and calls me Boulder. When she comes, she cries like she's breaking to pieces, she cries just like a rock.

Refusing would mean leaving her, so I ask for more time. I'll be forty soon, I don't have time, she says. Fucking milestones.

All I want is one goddamn week. The fact that I hadn't said yes the minute she asked seems to have exposed the tragic nature of our attachment, of that crushing thing people refer to as *the couple.* I come up with arguments and lay them on the table. A royal flush. We don't have time to look after a kid. The pregnancy would be high-risk. We'd be geriatric mothers, and by the time the kid went to high school, people would think we were the grandparents. The apartment's too small. Having a kid is the same as enrolling in a lifetime plan of suffering. Ridiculous arguments that never stood a chance against the urge they're trying to shoot down. We talk about it every day. She can't find it in herself to give me a week. She waits up for me and we drink coffee on the sofa. She looks at me with those blue eyes that fade to gray in the warm apartment light, and I have the feeling she has everything, that she is one and whole, like a god. That, somehow, her desire for a child spoils her. I listen with all five senses, I listen to her with my entire body, with everything but my heart, which feels like it wants to thrash the hell out of me. This wasn't a part of our plan. The truth is we'd never made any plans, we'd just taken huge bites out of life. I light a cigarette; I'm so despicable all I can think is that if she gets pregnant, I'll have to smoke outside the fucking building. She rests her head on my shoulders and closes her eyes. She takes shallow breaths, as if wanting to sigh but finding it too painful to draw in the oxygen contaminated by our conversation. She's nervous, receptive, she needs to hold in her belly the child she's found in her mind. Mostly, she's exhausted. I realize I'm part of her exhaustion, which is still better than not being part of her at all. I put my arm around her shoulders and my hand on her chest. She quietens down and curls into me. I kiss her hair out of inertia. Kisses that are tender and ready to sign a treaty. I am hooked on the smell of her, on the mix of shampoo and moisturizer that clings to her pajamas and skin, on the scent of every night in a decade spent folded around her sleeping body, of her success and her calm, even of our sad, awful morning sex. I tamp down the truth and say all right, let's do it. I don't tell her that what I want is to not be a mother.

The first person who had the idea of building a pyramid must have been insane. What about the guy who thought it made sense to stick someone in a rocket and shoot them at the stars? Samsa is crazier than the two of them put together. Having a kid is an enormous undertaking. It kicks into gear right away, without any warning. It comes out of nowhere with such extraordinary force that it razes everything to the ground, like an earthquake. You'd have to be an animal with a tiny brain and impeccable survival instincts to see it coming. I bet if we'd had a dog, it would've known long before any of us and cleared right out of the house. It seems unbelievable that a single decision, a fucking intangible thought, could so violently upset the flesh-and-bone scaffolding of daily life, the steady rhythm of the hours, the predictable, material color of the landscapes that give us nourishment and company. The decision precedes a living being that already exists and takes over everything. Its presence has dimension; it occupies the house with concrete tentacles, sinks into the skulls of the people who live there, and clings to the fine membrane that sheathes their gray matter. I can't get away, it follows me wherever I go like a sinner harassing another sinner, stoning him and hissing all of his fears into his ear. The decision hinges so much on me that it only sleeps when I do. Samsa, on the other hand, is radiant. She seems to generate a light whose source is the same active, powerful nucleus that glows inside a squid. When I look at her, she becomes younger and I have the feeling she's using my eyes as changing rooms in which to cast off the excess years and accomplish a purpose that will soon be expiring. Her lips have fleshed out the way they do on a person who's just done a lot of fucking, and she has the velvety gaze of a full-grown lioness that knows she is the backbone of the pride, the key to transcendence. I find it hard to believe a single idea could change her so much. When I bring her coffee in the morning, her hair shimmers over the pillow as if she were already pregnant.

Ragnar insists we have to celebrate. Here I was thinking we were friends. I tell him all I have to celebrate is the fact that I've reached new heights of stupidity, that I can't bring myself to hurt or leave Samsa, to understand the magnitude of her desire and say no. He tells me he felt the same when he had his first kid but that everything changes after the second or the third; they come out of their moms and grow up all on their own, all you have to do is feed them. He makes some dig that I can't remember about the food truck and slaps my back so hard I choke. I plan to pass the time smoking in a corner. Thankfully, he's a man of few words. Thankfully, too, he's the master of the bottles and shares them liberally. As we sit there surrounded by all those people getting drunk and having a great time, I feel as if we'd just won a battle and even though I'd lost an eye and one of my legs would have to be amputated, at least my heart was at peace and my courage intact.

I go with her to the clinic. It's a hideous building surrounded by other hideous buildings. They loom over the bay like gleaming icebergs that hold hostage ideas, ambitions, bodies. We can only see the tip: the law firms, the tech and IT companies, the corporations. The rest, most of which remains hidden, navigates the underseas of the third world. The fertility clinic is on the second floor of one of these glass-walled monsters. Samsa walks in resolute. She didn't have to ask, we both just assumed that wherever she went, I would go with her. A depressing prospect, but it is what it is. They show us into a waiting room. When she sits down, in her ironed blazer, with her perfect hair and made-up eyes, it's like she's taken possession of this new land and proclaimed herself Queen. It's always like this with her, I realize. The power she exudes is subtle, almost tender, beautiful and supple yet resilient, like the silk of a spider's web. She entices as much as she ensnares, lets you step back but never abandon her. She holds my hand and I light three cigarettes with my mind. I don't smoke, I fire them up and take a single long drag, burning through them without breathing. The chairs are comfortable. The magazines new. The floor pale and slick. The plants are so well tended they look fake. It's the perfect setting for her, and she fits in like it's her natural-born right. Another couple pushing forty sits across from us. Their clothes are clean, newly unfolded, and their hands held in accordance with some customary protocol. They're leafing through a magazine that claims to teach people how to be good mothers and fathers. The picture on the cover, a man and a woman with the vacant expressions of cult followers and a newborn baby in their arms, makes me feel sicker than the thought of Samsa being knocked up with a syringe and a sperm donation. We're going to have a massive problem if she ever brings home one of those how-to manuals. The kind you can pulp to death but still won't strain through the mesh of our love.

We get home with a list of chores and a hole in our checking account. I have the sense I am buying her a kid and that the approach I've taken is deceitful. I am frustrated, and it drains every last bit of my strength and talent. It's my biological impotence that coerces me, encourages me to do it. I feel like an elderly mafioso, like Samsa belongs to me not out of the love we have for one another but out of a new, shared responsibility, because I am in a position to accommodate an improbable, difficult whim. We run through the list that evening, curled up on the sofa. It's strange, we've never spent this much time on the sofa before. We'd bought it so her guests would have somewhere to sit, though we'd always made do with the bed. Lately, we end up here all the time. The sofa is a place for sitting and talking, a sensible piece of furniture designed to promote verticality and position the head as the sovereign supreme of all the subordinate organs, including the heart. I've developed an aversion toward it, I can't stand this heap of junk—not the sofa or the person I become whenever Samsa invites me to sit my ass down. I can't handle the square, navy-blue cushions crowded with other smaller cushions that are soft and garish and which she uses to buttress herself until she has the comfort she needs to control everything: her life, her feelings, the words she's already composing, even me. If every now and then she'd hug me the way she hugs those cushions, it might just melt the cold, rigid thing I carry inside and that bucks against me—because it couldn't care less about what I say or the promises I make. A barometer of circumstances, it makes me who I am: it can be shaped, but it won't be won over or driven away.

The chemical warfare begins. Samsa is the site of the conflict. Not only does she have her blood drawn several times, she also has to pop pills every morning: calcium, iron, folic acid, vitamins, iodine, estrogen. She reminds me of an abandoned warehouse suddenly beset by trucks come to unload their freight. Bricks, mortar, cement, beams, insulation, slabs. The impression I get is that she's eating the baby in chunks, little by little, and that once she's swallowed the last piece, the only thing left to do at the clinic will be to get their rubber stamp and press a button. We also have to fill a prescription at the pharmacy for a bunch of little bottles that are as precious as radium and just as hard to get hold of. A month later they arrive in a package that looks like a box of chocolates, the kind you don't want to throw away once it's empty. The glass vials are as tiny, slim, and adorable as perfume samples. Though they look like they hold water, they're actually full of hormones, the ferments that will activate life and deploy it when the time is right. After dinner, she's supposed to drain one with a very fine syringe, then inject it into the fat around her stomach. Every day for two weeks. She asks me if I'll do it; she can't, even though she's tried. She says that jabbing a ten-centimeter-long needle in her belly is as good as committing hara-kiri. The flesh she's pinching becomes taut and the hand holding the weapon refuses to obey; she is shielded by a biological mandate that makes her freeze up and stops the act of aggression. I've never done it before, but how hard can it be? I have her sit on the toilet. I sanitize her skin with a piece of gauze soaked in ethanol and tell her to focus on this baby she's been dreaming about so she can take the injection with dignity. She tells me to go to hell and I stick her with the needle, plunging the contents of the syringe into her body. It takes a second, all told. She says nothing and stares at me as if I'd just stabbed her. I'm dying to leave her there on her own. Instead I stay, kiss her forehead, kneel beside her, rest my head on her thighs, and apologize. A sense of calm falls over us like a shadowy canopy, making us feel lighter and closer together. It's cold, she complains as she touches the skin around the perforation. I want to remind her that the sperm she wants and needs so badly is preserved in liquid nitrogen, in the freezer. But I keep this thought to myself.

She eats all day. She has me bring home some empanadas, heads down to the grocery store and comes back loaded with cookies, cheese, and jars and jars of peanuts. The fact that the kitchen is too small for our needs seems to excite her. At night she pours herself a bowl of milk, crumbles a cinnamon stick into it. She devours it at the table, as absorbed by each spoonful as a tiger by a fresh carcass. The hormones are doing their job, they season and marinate her body, manipulating it to cater to the baby's taste and satisfaction. We visit the clinic every three days. They do an ultrasound and check the maturity of her eggs. I've learned that the sole purpose of these injections is to speed things up. The gynecologists' strategy is to reap Samsa's ovaries for all they're worth. If all goes according to plan, a week from now there will be eight to ten mature eggs where there'd usually be one. In other words, the ovary as overcrowded tenement. Then, just as soon as a batch of extraordinary possibilities has settled inside her, comes insemination. As they communicate this to us, she smiles. She's not even blinking, it's like she's been hypnotized. I can't believe she isn't changing her mind. Is she really going to let them pop her with an athletic twenty-year-old's forty to sixty thousand sperm? When there are *eight* mature eggs inside her? I voice my concerns with as much civility and composure as I can muster. I don't want to end up splashed across the front page of a newspaper with half a dozen babies crammed into a custom-made stroller looking pink and wrinkly as rats, while a woman with dark circles under her eyes stands beside me, wrecked on the inside and out. The gynecologist looks at Samsa and gestures in a way that conveys total understanding. Some forms of communication are both subtle and despotic, and have the power to isolate you from the conversation. Our great campaign has just become a precious, unfathomable thing hovering between the two of them. There's no room for me anymore. I'm the unwanted partner, a thing to be tolerated. Samsa makes her own feeble gesture. She's weak with embarrassment and can't come up with an excuse for my behavior. It's like my rationale is so crude it is an insult not only to her but to science, to the experimental approach, to the high priests of the holy church of insemination, who are ever so wise and down-to-earth, who are ever so pure.

The drive home is one of those rides where silence hangs around the car the way bloodlust does around soldiers, proud, zealous, in the seconds before combat. It consumes our bodies, gums them up and empties them of all kindness. Samsa drives in fits and starts, cleans the windshield twice, turns on the radio, says fucking bullshit, and turns it off. Meanwhile she won't stop gnawing on her cheeks, sucking at the insides of her mouth like she's trying to swallow them. She tends to do this when she's pissed off. That, and not talking to me, which would be great were it not for the fact that she usually runs out of steam and takes the opposite tack, which entails at least an hour of sofa-time. At a red light near the Reykjavík Art Museum, I decide to get out of the car. I tell her I have a lot of work to do. I slam the door and walk to the food truck. It's early, but I can work with the shutters down, pack the empanadas with more filling and elegantly mold the edges, creating a design that calls to mind Greek wall reliefs or the ridges down a dragon's back. I don't know, something. To spruce the day up a little, give it some part of me that will make it shine. As I take the key from my pocket and step into the truck, I feel like I am coming home. To a place of my own. It smells of yeast, cumin, pickled onions, and hot spices. When I close my eyes, I'm in another world—the always perfect world of the past, which nostalgia has wiped clean of every blemish and bruise.

I make sure to get home late, after she's fallen asleep. The fat and sugar in the milk she drinks mingle with her blood and send her into a deep slumber. It's been days since I went to the pub. Because of the whole business with the shots, I had to leave work early so I could be back in time for dinner and for the medical ritual needed for her to conceive. The door creaks a little. Silence. The lights are off—just a small, lone candle dying in the middle of a plate. I take off my coat and boots, shake off the snow, and tiptoe to the fridge. I open the freezer and grab a bottle. When you need to warm up after just having come out of winter's fist, you can either have a cup of hot coffee or a glass of cold brennivín. A long swig that scrapes down my throat like a match and starts a roaring fire in my arms and legs, as willful as a kid who thinks they can stay up all night. I'm not drunk, even though Ragnar was happy to see me and we kept coming up with reasons to toast each other. I'm not drunk, alcohol strips my tongue, gums, and mind, and leaves them sparkling. Alcohol is the friend that knows you have nothing to lose, holds you tight, and makes you feel like it's giving you everything. Its voice is a woman, the kind who can get you to laugh, an ally. I undress, leave my clothes on the floor, and crawl into bed. The intense heat of Samsa's body is rhythmic, it reaches my skin in waves that wash over me the way a murmuring tide washes over a lone rock, bringing in something new each time—a tale of shipwreck, a ship buried in the sand, calm and quiet at the bottom of the sea.

She wakes me in the middle of the night. She'd gotten up to go to the bathroom and can't fall back asleep. She says she needs to talk. I'm so tired and the thing she wants from me is so exhausting, I'd much rather fuck. All I have to do is think about it to know for a fact that it's an option—a road not as safe nor as traveled nor as flat, more like a shortcut, maybe, muddied and full of thorns, but on a horse that can deliver me unscathed to the other side. I don't have to tell her that I feel dumb. I don't have to make excuses for myself or listen to her or end up wrapped around her body, which grows bigger every day, satiating an insatiable hunger for feeling, for interest, for understanding. This is when I realize that sex is the easiest lie, because the thing we call *soul* and which seems to live in the shared chamber of love isn't real. It's not anything. Just a pair of devoted eyes. And they depend on the body—on the body and the brain, which know exactly how to imbue the eyes with passion. So it's easy to hush her by sucking on her neck and on her tongue and on her lips, by taking away her breath and killing her resolve. By staring into her eyes for ten minutes, fifteen, half an hour and sinking into her what she needs—words—as my hands give and take away desire and with it the bitterness and distress, drawing circles in the place where she is waiting for me, at the start and apparent end of the truth between us—which is to say, everything.

The long-awaited day has arrived. The gray December sky skims the ocean, swollen with pain. A restless calm threatens to stall over us like a ceiling, a thief of light heavy with toxins—lead, mercury, asbestos. Samsa doesn't even notice. She's having an Italian morning, her body is soft and full, she smells like fresh bread, like a sponge left in the sun, like tomato plants. She doesn't wait for me to bring coffee. She gets out of bed, has a shower, and carefully washes her body as if for the last time. When she steps out of the bathroom she's a whole new person—expansive and kind, breasts pushing against her purple sweater, the seams of her jeans all too visible, and her flesh, the new folds of her flesh trapped beneath them, straining. She's already a mother. She sits at the table and asks if I'd mind drinking her coffee. No more coffee, tobacco, or alcohol for her from now on. We'll need to stock up on tea and fruit juice. She grabs a stack of Post-its and starts writing out a new shopping list. She doesn't have much for breakfast, just a glass of milk and three biscuits. It's nerves, she says, but we should go out for dinner tonight to celebrate. It's been more than a decade and the woman inviting me out to dinner doesn't have a single cell in common with the woman who was eating lemon cake when I met her. Time has set its sights on us and slowly worn us down, sharpening its teeth on our bodies. I don't know what we are anymore. The strength of my body has been reduced to my body alone; I can't seem to see it in the things I say or do or need anymore. I unbutton my shirt near a mirror and the tattoo of Chiloé on my chest doesn't look real—just a parchment covered with made-up islands. Impossible routes only seem impossible because they're dangerous. The solitary ones—those we pay for with our lives.

# 3

The streets crack through the vellum of ice that formed overnight and emerge one by one, like a flotilla of submarines, wherever traffic begins to form. First the thoroughfares—Hringbraut, Kringlumýrarbraut, Sæbraut—and little by little the streets, the small squares, the alleyways. Ten to nine. The morning is a gloomy, hungover teenager still in bed at eleven thirty. Samsa is relaxed as she drives. Yesterday she picked out the music she wanted to listen to on the way there and back. Today has to be perfect, fragrant with perfume and fruit, like an apple tree. We park in our usual spot and bundle up. She holds me there for a few seconds with a sudden kiss that is both too long and too wet for a car kiss. We get out and she takes my hand. She's excited. I get the impression she wants to include me in what she's going through, that she is doing it out of consideration, not for her but for me. It's as if she can see the contours of the infidelity that lurks behind the curtains of what she's about to do, and wants to hide it from me, to protect herself. She touches me so I feel present, so my mind believes the impossible: That what they are going to do to her they are also doing to me, that the burden of our decisions is a singular thing, and bearable when shared.

. . .

At the door, I tell her to head on inside; I want to smoke a cigarette. She smiles and says she'll see me in a bit. She's all body today, all liquid and ember, cells and welcome—everything leaves her feeling warm and motivated. She disappears and I'm left on my own, under the harsh glow of the front entrance. I decide to do a lap around the building. I light my cigarette and walk in the half-dark. It dawns on me that when life plows into the anvil of winter, the things it casts out let off clouds of steam. Buildings and vehicles and people, containers and ships and birds, even the off-limits strips of vegetation. Morning lifts their warmth, waking them. This is how it chooses to summon them and take hold of them and help them adjust to a new day, entering it with just enough force to make it turn and forge ahead. I walk and smoke. I don't think, I observe. I realize it's hard to observe without thinking, to take things at face value, to let the eyes drink it all in and let it all out, to shut down the mind. I give it a shot, I succeed. The secret is to discredit yourself first—before, long before, you discredit the miracles imposed by life, that beggarly saint.

Samsa is the first wager of the day. Her three mature eggs are all lined up at the starting gate, perfect little seeds. A lesbian in a fertility clinic is a safe bet. A body that's never been put to the test, flawless, authoritative, free of all disappointment and frustration. Samsa knows this. She could have gotten pregnant just by touching the designated semen with her fingertips, by sniffing it, drinking it, letting it melt on her belly like an ice cube in summer. Three mature eggs to ensure a successful conception. There's a high chance two of them will be fertilized. The seasickness I never felt on the ocean now cruises through my body and takes a leak on my brain. I don't know where I am, but it isn't here with the woman I love, stroking her cheek as she relaxes on the hospital bed, naked from the waist down, her sex covered in a hospital sheet that doesn't know the meaning of sleep. They leave us alone for a few minutes. On the wall, not far from the ceiling, is a TV. The images flashing on it leave me speechless. It's the BBC, a road somewhere in the Middle East. Ruins, dust, a man dressed in rags running for his life. Sharpshooters. The screen is out of reach and there aren't any chairs for me to climb on to turn it off. The fact that someone else's incompetence has driven me to play a part I hate not only offends me, it pisses me off. I stick my head out of the door and call in the first nurse that walks by. Samsa has closed her eyes and breathes as though she has been left alone and there were no other world but the one inside her, which is unique, beautiful and carefree, inviolable. I tell the woman that if she doesn't turn that garbage off right that second, I'll have to take my partner somewhere else. She runs out, and soon a dizzying zap has turned the streets of Benghazi into a garden of honeysuckle abuzz with tiny blue hummingbirds whose beaks are a pair of fine tweezers and whose angry, beady eyes are like those of a person with no choice but to eat on their feet. Samsa looks at me and laughs. She says thank you. I need to get the hell out of here. I need a cigarette, a whole fucking bottle of brennivín, a boat in the harbor with a hollow in the keel for me to hide in.

An hour later, we head back to the apartment. I drive because Samsa doesn't want to open her legs. I don't know why I get the feeling I'll be driving a lot from now on. At home, she asks me to fuck her. Right now? She says orgasms increase the likelihood of conception. I don't know how to make her understand that all her eggs have probably been fertilized at this stage. Artificial insemination is a revolutionary act, 100 per cent democratic. The syringe piston shoots the sperm straight into a nest full of eggs. They don't have to cross a desert, and it isn't the final leg of a race, the bravest swimming shoulder to shoulder with the slackers, the idlers, and the idiots. Fate is inside, noble and reckless, dealing its cards with a blindfold over its eyes. It's a lottery, like anything else. Still, she insists. Postcoital contractions can be key to monetizing the capital we've invested in this venture. Postcoital contractions. Capital. Venture. I fuck her the way she wants me to, with cold precision, to escape the substance of her words. To kill the conversation.

She has an appointment in fifteen days for another set of tests. She doesn't eat for several hours before leaving the house. Then they draw her blood again. Blood, the snitch everyone hates. It keeps you alive on one condition: transparency.

It creeps around the body like a shrewd domestic who has access to every room and knows everything there is to know about you. And who talks under pressure. The body is too basic, too weak; it can't be trusted. Only the mind can console us for its disloyalty; the only flag it flies is that of freedom, made of the bones of truth and the bones of lies—a cross; white against black. Blood respects nothing.

I know the moment I see her. She jogs across the square, hand pinning her coat to her chest, no scarf or gloves on. She laughs. Her hair hangs loose. She hasn't straightened it, and it ribbons in the gray morning light, giving her the rebel look of an artist, spontaneous and impulsive. Her hair looks like it's about to self-immolate, a bundle of twigs that huddles together the second before the fire is lit. I wish she was always like this. Alive and in motion. Amazingly feverish and present. By the time she reaches the food truck she's panting. She scares the clientele by ordering two empanadas at the top of her lungs, one for her and one for the baby. Just two? Just one baby? Yes. If I'd ever disowned a god, now would be the time to peel off strips of my skin and offer up the fat of my body as an oblation. I get out of the food truck, hold her, then kiss her with unprecedented, disproportionate feeling. Given that I'll be living my life on a high tightrope, maybe this fetus is the thing I need to help balance out my strength and my angst, the risk of plummeting into the void and the possibility that I might reach terra firma at any moment. Any other outcome would have caused a storm where there is now a silent, tolerable calm, the kind of uneventful voyage that needs no captains, officers, or mechanics. Not even sailors.

I'd always thought of pregnant women as just women with bellies swollen to the size of dwarf planets. Now I know that's not all it is. A visibly pregnant woman is a pregnant woman who has experience. She's already gone through the learning process that sets her apart and honors her with the attention of the other's gaze. A visibly pregnant woman is like an ancient witch; she guards the secret to life, and this makes her more than human, nearly semidivine. Her energetic body is an enormous mouth that speaks on her behalf, regardless of whether anyone is listening. But a newly pregnant woman, a woman in her first trimester . . . Now she's a hand grenade, a ticking bomb that sleeps beside you. Her uterus is the sensor that holds the diamond, it's a reactor, it contains the Big Bang, a surplus of neutrons and nitroglycerin. The smallest disturbance can set it off. Samsa changes dramatically. It's as though her primary root had been grafted onto that of a toothless but ravenous vegetal being that uses her to feed on the life sap of others. One second she wants me, the next she rejects me; one second her heart fucking brimmeth over and I have to swallow every word and feeling that pours out of her, the next she isn't talking to me at all. She needs me and she ignores me, sometimes in quick succession, constantly, in the space of a single afternoon. If I play along, she gets angry. When I put her in her place, she turns on the waterworks, as if crying were one of those infections that drives you to suddenly empty your stomach, to throw up until you run out of breath. Hashish, cocaine, synthetic drugs—what a farce. There are hormone concentrations that can shoot you up to the sky and then drive you into the arms of the most unhinged Furies—not the kind that read you your sins but the kind that machinate them. This is the unexplainable daily routine of the bellyless pregnant woman, heroes who cultivate life at the expense of their own, with no bearing on anything or anyone outside their immediate surroundings, their partner and their home. What's left of Samsa? When she comes back from work, she gets undressed, showers, then has something to eat and to drink. It's like having a woodland creature running around the house, touching and snuffling everything with its little, burrowing nose. We talk and fuck and lie on the sofa watching TV, Samsa with her feet up and her head in my lap. When I run my fingers through her hair, I don't have the courage to breathe. She's in charge now, the one who starts conversations and ends them, who wants me and knows exactly how I should want her. She is told as much by the tyrannical, still-brainless thing inside her, which robs her of all reason while at the same time branding a lesson of undying allegiance onto the hungry, pliant walls of her uterus, where no other person in the world can leave their mark.

Time flies for Samsa. For me, it's never moved more slowly. I'm the girl who promised she'd be good for a year. After that, we'd have to see. I changed the opening hours for the food truck. I don't close as late anymore and head straight home. Now and then I poke my head into the pub, but it's always early and Ragnar's still setting up in the kitchen. What can you do. Samsa, on the other hand, is busier than ever. She's signed up for a childbirth class and a course in prenatal water aerobics that almost cost us our relationship. She wanted me to come with her. Apparently, most of the women bring their partners. They pretend to be whales while their plus-ones hold them by the armpits. All of this in a small, temperate pool. Awesome bellies with outies like the stubborn knots on balloons, insectivorous swimming caps, bodies that once loved themselves with abandon now soft and vulnerable as they bob on the cottony water, anchored by the tentacles. In spite of it all, something still touches them and drives them forward, the same something that makes them smile dumb-mouthed like those deluded terminal patients who die convinced that they are living. Naturally, I said I wouldn't go, and Samsa spat out her special brand of poison—the kind that doesn't kill but leaves you blind, that erases your best memories and replaces them with a chasm for you to trip into and leave behind the skin of your knuckles and knees, of your confidence. I didn't go home that night. I got drunk with Ragnar and was happy like those people who use alcohol to chip away at themselves until they've exposed the layers underneath, the bedrock on which we erect our public-facing life. The real one—about as real as the artist whose reflection is painted into a corner of their own minor work.

. . .

We make peace when I promise to go to childbirth class with her. I'm not a fan, but it's one of the various unsavory appetizers I knew I'd have to swallow when I agreed to the pregnancy, like attending prenatal appointments and being there for the birth itself, or browsing for strollers and helping pick out the creature's first set of clothes. The classes are a bit like ultrasound appointments: they generate high expectations and the results are at best confusing. You either need a hangover or an active imagination to be able to appreciate them. Samsa attends each one as if it were a religious event. She bought an outfit for the occasion, baggy at the thighs, with a lot of spandex around the belly and ankles. She sets an alarm on her phone to make sure we're not late and puts her hair up before leaving the house. I'd be interested to know why she also takes off her make-up. During these forty-five-minute sessions it dawns on me that pregnant women are like seeded plots, like farm animals. I could swap out Samsa for any of the others. She's in her seventh month. I don't know where she's gone to; I touch her and she's not there; she has become the thing inside her; she is pliant, subject to a constant manufacturing process that outstrips and unravels her. The classes make me very uncomfortable. The worst part isn't the bodies or the instructions of the midwife, who is there to help the women blossom and open up. No, the worst part is the cloth of complicity woven together by the looks that pass between partner and partner, between pregnant woman and pregnant woman. There is a heft that holds this construction together—the shared consciousness of a group, an order, something like a caste. You have the chosen ones, with their unfinished, centaur-like fruits inside them, and their protectors, a kind of human connection with the real, nonessential world. The midwife is a guru who urges us to straddle peanut balls while we control our breathing and eye one another with condescension. The whole thing is so unsettling I wish I could trade it in for a mortar and pestle or a punching bag. This is the hardest exercise: to stay calm as the current pulls you under and fills your guts with substances that are impossible to digest. To stand tall, like an outcrop in the middle of the ocean, so eroded you can't tell from a distance whether you're looking at a dead animal bobbing in the water or a rock clamoring for air.

We've stopped fucking. Samsa is sexless, a dockyard gridlocked by a single ship. She devotes every second of night and day to the project that demands her attention. A fine-mesh filter barricades the mouth of her desire. There's nothing left of her for me, she's transformed. She won't even let me touch her. She won't let me use her without pretending to give something back, just to satisfy the hunger that has accumulated inside me after a week of rejections. When I masturbate next to her in bed, she turns away, as though wanting to protect the child from something ugly, from the inherent wickedness of bodies that don't understand the virtue of growing a new life, bodies that do nothing but spread their failings and their fears, their insatiable thirst for warmth and approval. I touch myself and every part of me falls, I retreat to the place where I've summoned my body. I'm a winter flower that bloomed by mistake and closes again.

Every orgasm is a small funeral. When I finish, she waits a minute before turning to face me again. She takes my hand and places it on her stomach. This must be how the gods felt the day the continents knocked heads and formed mountains. My hand is impotence itself. I feel nothing. I close my eyes and rest.

According to the gynecologist, Samsa will give birth in ten to fifteen days. She doesn't wait up for me in the evenings anymore. The baby needs Samsa asleep so that it can suck up the final dregs of her existence. She has stopped going to work, she's been on maternity leave for weeks. She wakes up late every morning, nods off a couple of times during the day, and goes to bed around dinner. I've even thought that if the kid doesn't come out by the due date, Samsa might fall into a coma and be consumed by the baby, who would drain her from head to toe, leaving behind only the useless husk of her skin. I don't know why I have the feeling that if this were to happen, the baby would crawl out of her mouth. A mouth like a snake's, jaw unhinged. I don't share my theories with her. Instead I go out drinking with Ragnar. I call Samsa in the late afternoon to make sure she's okay and wish her a restful sleep, then work until after midnight. It's September again, everyone's hungry, and the nightlife here never stops. The country can't seem to decide whether it needs or even wants those endlessly dark winter months in which to carry out with impunity all the thoughts that were incubated in the forensic light of day. I lower the shutters, grab a bag of empanadas, and head to the pub. We're like dogs, Ragnar and me. Always happy to see each other. We hug tightly, and he hands me a bottle. He's been drinking for a while and his eyes are opalescent, like ice cubes at the bottom of a glass, tinged with a slow disquiet that draws me in. I sit and have a drink with him. Ah, the old days! The old days are always better. The present knows this and chooses to punish us out of jealousy. The mood in the pub is dank, dusky, and loud; it holds me and questions me at the same time. If I'm anyone, it's this person. If peace is taking a breath and not feeling your ribs, my peace is here and it is very simple. It lives in my fingers, trickles into the palm of my hand, and travels under my clothes. I've found it again, the balmy touch of its tiny paws is both thrilling and soothing. We raise our glasses without a word and something vital passes between our eyes, something that lives deep inside us, like a hand that scratches and cannot be burned or corroded by words.

I smoke one last cigarette before heading up to the apartment. The harbor is stunning at night, a glistening strip with glinting yellow and orange lights. They look like a troupe of dancing ghosts that refuse to go to bed and call for an uprising. It must look even more beautiful from the ocean. I shut my eyes for a minute and arrive in Puerto Montt, a slow, spectacular entrance into one of the most beautiful bays in the world, wide as a public square and clean as the sky. Seen from the boat, the city looked like the façade of a large hotel at night. The first time we docked there, I didn't disembark. Instead I sat on the deck for hours, taking it all in. I wish I'd known how to play the guitar, wish I could've whispered it a slow tune, described its beauty and spoken its name. Puerto Montt was one of our usual stops, and we went back several times. That was where I bought Samsa her first pendant. I used to give her jewelry inlaid with unusual stones that she recognized the moment she saw them. I'd buy them in places hundreds of miles away, and store them in my cabin for weeks. When I held them in my hand, it was like I was holding her, flush with warmth. They gave me sustenance, those stones. Like when you latch onto a memory so substantial you can go without supper because it's already filled every corner of your body.

Samsa is overdue. We've been told that if she doesn't go into labor in four days, they'll have to induce. The baby has fetal macrosomia. If only you could set fire to every word that evokes an illness. Samsa puts her hands on her belly and I grow several layers of rust, one on top of the other; I age all at once. I've just learned that a child's diagnosis can kill you too. The gynecologist is a borderline psychopath. For a second he savors the waves of turbulence caused by his epistemic assault. Then he becomes a doctor again. Lunatics can be some of the most soft-spoken people in the world—they speak like a mother who knows everything and cuts to the bone. Fetal macrosomia is when the baby is larger than normal, he explains. I breathe. It's a fucking Icelandic fetus inside the body of an Icelander who's spent the past nine months downing pints of milk and stuffing herself with cheese. No wonder the kid is massive. Samsa gets up from her chair and says the baby will come out when it's ready, not a second before. She grabs her purse, fixes her eyes on me, nods once, and leaves.

We haven't had to go to war with the hospital. Instead, we're having the baby at home. I don't think it's a good idea but I'm not the one who's going to lose buckets of blood, Samsa calls the shots. The midwife arrives just as the first contractions begin. The real ones. The ones that remind me that we have neighbors with phones and a direct line to the cops. They say midwives lose track of time. My sense of it distorts. Twelve hours of agony. Each a day long. Samsa screams like a patient at a mental asylum. She starts at the top of her lungs, without warning, and stops just as suddenly. This happens over and over, minute after minute. She doesn't talk, she howls. She doesn't breathe, she pants. Even though the midwife brought a million things with her, she keeps asking me for stuff. I warm up hot compresses in the microwave, boil water, toss out underpads, brew herbal teas, rummage through the pots and pans until I find one big enough to throw up in. It becomes clear to me how imperfect nature is. Imperfect and cruel, almost furious. It's not wise and never has been. How many centuries have to pass before a woman can give birth without it looking like an experiment? The midwife keeps a cool head. She asks the baby to flow and Samsa to flow with it. All I can think about are cesareans. I am witnessing something reckless. Like stealing jewels from a museum or breaking prisoners out of a police van—there's just so much that can go wrong. Every second contains a possible mistake. Danger sticks out its tongue and coats everything in a layer of gluey, lethal drool. Samsa calls me over and crushes the bones in my hand. She asks me if I love her. There's something exacting in her voice. Her eyes are blank and she looks like she's high. I tell her that I love her, of course I do, more than anyone in the world. The words tumble out of me, like I'd heard them a million times on the same TV show. Then she swears at me and tells me to leave her alone, she doesn't want to see my face. The midwife says it's normal, that she's under the influence of hormones that are out of control. She talks about Samsa like she's not there in the room with us, or as if she spoke a foreign language. It's so surreal, I've lost all awareness of my body—of thirst, exhaustion, hunger. Samsa fills everything around her and sucks up the whole world like a black hole. Three more hours. She's fully dilated, the midwife says as she polishes off a banana. Samsa had wanted to deliver the baby in a squatting position, but she can't take it anymore; her pain is a well-trained fist, and it's knocked her down. Without meaning to, my eyes drift to her vagina. I don't know what it's supposed to look like. A fistful of raw flesh, the gaping wound of an animal that has no hope left and is bleeding to death. The midwife says the baby is so big it can't even settle into position, that it has to come out all at once, in a single, good push. I'm about to call an ambulance when Samsa's moaning changes. She doesn't sound like a woman anymore. She is an animal, a dragon, a beast capable of laying waste to everything in a single flaming breath. The midwife calls me over. I go. I don't know where I am, I am no one. A crown kisses the light for the first time. Someone pulls at the body so that it won't get stuck. I hold it in my arms. The baby breathes. Gives off heat. Has weight. A tiny miracle, at once the hardest and softest thing in the world. The eyes open. It's a girl. She looks at me. I feel myself die a little.

# 4

Samsa's motherhood is exclusive. It has no bearing on me; I've been sent into exile. She and Tinna are still one, just like when Samsa was pregnant. They spend all day lying on the sofa with no clothes on, skin touching skin. Her life has been reduced to breastfeeding. Tinna has a nipple in her mouth at all times. It's her bottle, her pacifier, her toy. She never gets tired of it. Samsa's nipple belongs to Tinna as much as the tongue and the palate that press down on it. When she falls asleep and it slips away from her, it's as if the sun had slipped away from its planet: the cold is absolute, and so monstrous it wakes her up, sending her into a panic. She headbutts Samsa, mouth open like a massive eye that wants to take back all of its sanity and light. If she can't find it, she screams. She has her own special way of screaming, unlike that of any other baby in the world. Her screams are a swarm of locusts that raze everything, raze everything and then leave. I'm terrified of them. Of the nothingness they leave in their wake, the ground leveled with bodies. Samsa, on the other hand, finds it all delightful, she's reached some kind of nirvana. Nothing bothers her, not the cracks in her nipples, which sting and bleed, not the cramps that make her double over, not even when I overcook the pasta. She watches TV, eats whatever I put in front of her, and whispers to Tinna, hidden under the duvet with the baby draped over her body, as if they'd both decided to have a sleepover and it were now time to share secrets. I don't stop still. I cook, I do the shopping, I clean. I don't get how a baby who does nothing but loll around naked all day and who eats from a tit can triple the house chores. I don't understand a thing. Whenever I take out the trash, I sit on the steps and rest for a while. I light one cigarette with another. I don't want to think. I feel used, I feel isolated, I feel spent. I don't like this life. It's the life of a seasonal worker, a serf. Better not to think. Under these circumstances, thinking isn't just dangerous—it's dumb.

We've moved. After witnessing its first family be pushed out by five kilos' worth of baby, the little yellow house now bolts down our belongings. Everything fits—the four pieces of furniture from our old apartment, the contents of Samsa's wardrobe, my kitchen equipment, and all of Tinna's ridiculous clutter. She's two months old. Two months isn't nearly enough time to have hoarded so much wealth. Ragnar helps with the move. Between us, we load everything into his van. I don't know why I'm embarrassed by Tinna's things. All manner of recliners and chairs with safety rails and straps, belts and wheels. Bags filled to the top with baby clothes. Cardboard boxes small and large with little plastic windows that open onto pastel-colored gadgets—some of them electric, most of them ergonomic, all of them nonessential. Toys meant to shape the baby's brain, organic-cotton dolls, small blocks of wood contrived by a child development specialist. I touch everything. Her belongings pass through my hands like suitcases along a conveyor belt. I grab them, move them, dispose of them. They've got nothing to do with me. Samsa is at the pool with Tinna. They've signed up for a swimming class for babies. I thought she was joking when she told me. She wasn't. Apparently, babies can swim underwater. They learn in their mother's uterus, but then life makes them cry and then immediately makes them breathe, and before you know it they've forgotten. Samsa doesn't want this to happen, as if giving Tinna life hadn't been enough and it was now her responsibility to manage it. Is this what mothers do? String up invisible nets, preside over their child's safety? I'm the one who had to learn how to breathe. I knew it straight away. The moment she was inseminated, Samsa changed. The feeling I had was one of unfamiliarity—an anxious, nomadic unfamiliarity that came from Samsa. It took over her while at the same time soaking through her and turning her radioactive—as if those mobile vials of life, that freshly brewed soup of despair, had also somehow inoculated her. The birth hasn't changed a thing; it hasn't absolved her or brought her back to me. She hasn't budged an inch: motherhood is the tattoo that defines you, brands life on your arm, the mark that impedes freedom.

The feeling of emptiness is so large, I'd wear blinders if I could—a scrap of leather at each temple to make sure

I hew to the well-traveled, clear-cut future unfolding before me. Living life by killing myself slowly. Is that all it takes? There are too many oceans receding from too much land. There are too many fossils inside rocks, too much life left to declare. It might be more effective to cover my ears than to white out my eyes, because until now I've let my eyes make decisions for my brain, and no other organ inside me has the courage to stand up to the trumpet whose vibrato has bored straight into my feeling. I need to swim with the tide—use up my maternity leave, go back to work, wait for Samsa to get her act together, to realize there are parts of herself that she misses, then win them back and make them fit the woman she's become, who doesn't live for herself anymore but who lives through the person trapped in the body of a baby girl who smiles and wants her and has her wrapped around her little finger with a force that can't be matched, because it belongs to the stars and the earth. In other words, to no one.

The kitchen in the new house is awkward. There are six burners, an oven, a steam oven, an inconvenient island, and handleless furnishings from top to bottom and right to left. Before we moved, Samsa made a trip to IKEA and ransacked the cookware and tableware section. We keep it all hidden in the cupboards. Handsome, brand-new cutlery that doesn't speak to me and that I don't see the point in. We have breakfast at a table next to the window. Scrambled eggs, buttered toast, cranberry juice, and a pot of tea. Autumn serves us its final mornings. I enjoy these hours of prelude—unfolding the tablecloth, lighting the candles, feeling like every part of what I do is being written into a time of solitude that belongs entirely to me, and written into the minutes I carefully weave together with every movement of my tactful fingertips. Time doesn't live outside us; it comes into being as we do. To be able to hold time in our hands—now that's a human mission. When I wake up the house still bobs in silence, a sleeping rowboat sheltered by other boats, a wooden box where everything seems to begin and end. I don't turn on any lights. Samsa sleeps far away from me, at the other end of the world, glued to Tinna's crib, which has a detachable rail that clips onto the bed. Sleeping this close to two people who love each other is worse than sleeping alone. I pull on a sweater and head down to the kitchen. I haven't woken up, what I've done is made my escape. When Samsa shows up two or three hours later with Tinna all dressed and happy, something there, in the hollow of my chest, doesn't feel right, like an ancient leak or the murmur of a gust of wind that rushes past, its prophecy inaudible.

I made a mistake and went to one of Samsa's private meetings. A traveling breastfeeding group. There are between ten and fifteen mothers. Like lancers, they each come armed with a baby. They meet once a week at the home of one of the moms, where they chat and breastfeed their infants. Then came our turn. Samsa wakes up shortly after I do and does something unprecedented: she hands me Tinna, already full and fed. She puts her in my arms and tells me to change her diapers and get her dressed, that she's left the clothes laid out on the changing table. For once she has too much on her plate, all of which makes the baby an inconvenience. She has to shower, brush her hair, put on make-up to look presentable, slip into her nursing clothes—not her outside clothes or loungewear but a top fastened at the chest with a ribbon that when undone unleashes her breasts, which have never looked so full or out of reach. Samsa makes sure I've understood, then leaves. Silence. An underwater, hospital-like silence. It's my first time one-on-one with Tinna. We give each other curious looks, as if our faces somehow seemed familiar, as if we recognized each other from a place we can't seem to put our fingers on. I explain what we'll be doing and lay her down on the changing table. She doesn't make a peep. She moves her legs and arms the whole time, like a beetle that has rolled onto its back. She flails with such passion she starts to pant. Then she finds the clothes Samsa had picked out for her and kicks them onto the floor. She makes me laugh. The ensemble, a white knitted dress with pink socks, isn't my cup of tea either. You know what? We can pick something else out. I take her in my arms and we head to the dresser. I like walking around the room with her, smelling the very fine layer of skin at the top of her head, sniffing her with my lips and holding onto her warmth. When you're inside a house with a baby awake in your arms, you instinctively search for the windows. Tinna's eyes gaze into the distance, drawn to the light that bounces off the ocean. They fix on it as if on a miracle, as though sunrise were a phenomenon that only came about every ten centuries. I think she might be on to something, actually. I can't remember the last time I sat still, eye to eye with the swell of light that swallows up the sky every day and presents it to us.

The doorbell. Loud chattering at the entrance winds into the house and settles in. Some human voices are annihilating. I hug Tinna to my body for a second, then finish getting her dressed. She fusses because she doesn't like to be jostled around. I sing. I'm not sure exactly what, I hum a song I must have heard on the radio, a Latin tune that makes her body tense up, as though ready to dance. Samsa calls me. She probably wants the baby back, living proof of her reign. I muss her hair, which looks like it's been sewed onto her head, and give her two kisses, one on the nose and one on the forehead. Grudgingly, I walk downstairs. I feel as if a merciless god has just asked me to give up my daughter. What does it take to banish a god? Isn't it enough to simply not believe? Samsa has stuffed all of our chairs and armchairs into the living room. There's a table in the middle, with various baked goods and beverages, nipple shields and underpads. Kilos and kilos of women and their babies. They sit down and undress. Icelandic heating cranked up all the way as always. Their large breasts hang loose, one hand guiding a tit to the baby's mouth. They laugh, nurse, and eat, all while looking at each other, touching each other, drawing comparisons. Nipples in every size, some small as berries, others wide and dark like bread. Eager little tongues lick and stimulate them. Now I get why Samsa never misses a single one of these get-togethers. They're orgies. They share the same excesses, the same extravagance, the same body and bodily pleasure that are heightened when experienced as one. Samsa takes Tinna and asks why I've dressed her in a pair of pirate pants and a shirt that doesn't match. She hisses this at me with a quiet rage that is both unfamiliar and unsurprising. I look at her and say nothing. All I can do is swear back at her, but her motherhood is bulletproof. She pats Tinna's hair down with one hand and takes her to the armchair. I run out of the house.

I spur each day on as if it were the beast that carried my load. Home, grocery store, work, home again. That's not true. Between leaving work and going home, I've been stopping at the pub. At first I didn't want to. I used to picture evenings in our living room, slow-footed as fado, with Tinna crawling along the carpet like a snail through thick grass—stubborn, halting, relentless. Tinna and me and her basket of toys. But I haven't been able to make it happen. Samsa is always around, watching us, possessed. She's given up her life, found religion. Her motherhood is just that, a tiered system of values that aspires to encompass and clarify everything. I confront her about it one night when I come home late after drinking with Ragnar. Samsa lies in bed, crying. She's a victim, a body felled by the emotions that wash her hair with tears. I tell her I'm not cut out to be a mother, much less a lapdog, the obedient company she wants from me. We look at each other in the half-dark. The streetlights are movie-like, they outline the dark shadows of our bodies, coloring them blue, emptying them completely. Tinna is asleep right where her mattress fastens to ours, trusting and calm. Silken eyelashes, warm nostrils that are clean and light, as if just written. She breathes and it's like she's made of wax—a doll. I want to swoop in through the window and snatch her away, to punish Samsa for being close-minded and weak. For isolating me from Tinna—and from her. Samsa's arguments are biological: it's the hormones, it's the symbolic cord, it's the breastfeeding. She has the nerve to allege that the baby's first year belongs to the mother, she read it somewhere. *Que et fotin.* I've also made a commitment to motherhood, not because I needed a kid but out of love for Samsa. Now that I've made the commitment, it's all I want. We end up fucking, for too many reasons. Because she feels powerful and I feel alone. Because love leaves a residue and residues have memories. Because she feels guilty. Because I spent all night making eyes at another woman and now I'm horny. Fucking for these reasons is the same as leaving a burning building through the emergency exit, down a stairwell that leads nowhere.

We've come to an agreement. An explicit one that gets me Wednesdays with Tinna. Samsa concedes there's some truth to my claim. She says she mulled it over all night, while sleeping. She gets up and the bed is no longer a bed but a throne. She nurses Tinna, then hands her over. She has invited me into her domain—back squared, neck never exposed, on her head a tiara made of tresses and teeth. Tinna comes to me like something borrowed. Samsa has just unbuttoned her pajamas and smiles. She's a mountain towering before me, a natural border suitable only for animals, packed with death and snow. Her law is mineral, which means there's nothing to be done—no threats or tactics I can resort to, no movement that can shake her. I can love and admire her because she entices me, because she is a crush of impractical beauty that I barrel into with pleasure, doing myself no harm. She feels magnanimous today as she lifts up her daughter and gives her to me. She knows she's invincible. Somewhere there is a list of the names of women and mountains like Samsa. They are complete beings, and I am scared of this fullness, which throws my shortcomings into sharp relief. I hold Tinna the way I would hold a bag of gold, knowing that from now on no matter where I go, the treasure that is in my care and that I am not allowed to spend will be written all over my face.

Life has started to wind down. Something intangible compels me from the moment I wake up. I enter every day the way an explorer enters charted land—bored and incautious. They don't interest me. Tinna grows with determination, as though doing so gives her freedom. She gets up, unfurls—it's like she's opening up little by little and letting out a stream of light that lifts all the ugliness from the world. The house is her planter. Samsa feeds her. I'm the bird that comes by for a visit and sings because the sight of her makes me happy. I had no idea a child could be such a huge obstacle. Everything around me looks calm, and yet there are no open passages. I am under the thumb of a live, proliferating force that prevents me from leaving and threatens to sever my body, which wants to escape, from my head, which was made to stay.

We sleep in separate bedrooms. I used to think this kind of thing only happened with grandparents or with couples that snore. But apparently babies are light sleepers and, unless you're the mother, even the smallest movement or sound can wake them. At least according to Samsa, who's tired of being woken by Tinna five or six times a night so she can be nursed. She says I'm a violent sleeper, that when I thrash about on the mattress it's like I'm exorcising my demons. I'm sick of the extrasensory powers that biology confers on its devotees, but at the same time I don't have the energy to argue about nonsense. I grab my pillow, some candles, and an ashtray and move into the guest room. Lying in bed at ten thirty in the morning. The striped sheets new and unwashed. The mattress never slept in. I could've gone to Tinna's room, which is right next to ours and has already been fitted for her arrival in some four or five years, which is around the time people in Japan think it's okay for the baby to sleep alone without being traumatized by the experience of solitude. Instead I chose this room, the junk room. It's the smallest one, north-facing. It's where we keep the ironing board, and the still-unopened moving boxes. They're unlabeled and may as well be empty. Strange, this is the only room I feel at home in. Here I am again in the company of the short term—a great talker and an excellent listener. Here I am again on a bunk bed—between one port and another.

# 5

Like illness, celibacy makes us more human. It's not that it takes hold of my body. No. It takes over my body's temperament. I can feel it burrowing, leaving a perfectly round hole; I can sense it tunneling into me until it's found the perfect place to build a nest. That's where the lack of sex—like a cluster of viruses or worms—pitches its house and begins to gnaw away at me. I am its support system, and the void expands and grows stronger with my help, switching skeletons several times, laying hundreds of eggs, incubating them. It prevails over me the way biological mothers prevail over everything, through reproduction. But all this tunneling has opened rifts through which the captive parts of me have started to emerge. I realize that I am smoke, that the things that define me rise as they would up a chimney, probing every crack, searching for a wellspring of light or cold, a cupola of sky to sprawl into. I don't mean my personality. Personality is a dress made of scraps that I never stop washing or mending; it clothes me, might even suit me, but it will never, ever define me. The nakedness I conceal is what makes me a person. Skin, my sweeping prairieland. The absence of sex has undressed me and I have seen myself. I have seen and recognized myself the way someone who is blind might recognize a breathful of salt air rising at sundown from the bowels of the sea.

She often comes by for an empanada, around lunchtime, like everyone else, a couple of times a week. She is not a typical Icelander; body lithe and muscles slender like an athlete's. Her face is pristine, her bangs perfect, and her eyes an unusual shade of green, dark and opaque like malachite. She has the look of a curator, and probably works at the Art Museum or the National Gallery. She always orders the same thing, the empanada of the day and a long black. I don't understand why she has such an effect on me. It's as if every word she says were slow-dancing out of her mouth bent on seducing me. Sometimes seeing her in the distance is enough to me make me feel intractable. I recognize desire, a castaway resurfacing energized and feral from a journey embarked on long ago. I surrender to it, because feeling this desire means feeding its oceans, filling my cunt with sea foam, stringing my neck with pearls that make me bend at the knee. I feel fucking incredible when she moves her lips just to talk to me. I wrap the empanada, make her coffee, seal it, ring her up. I hand her the bag and we look at each other, all it takes is a second. Her nails, which I would swallow one by one, are so shiny they look inhuman.

Wednesdays are my weekends. Samsa gets up early and makes herself scarce. She has somehow managed to squeeze into a single day all the leisure of her old life: Spanish lessons, painting classes, yoga, gym, lunch with friends. You'd have to be hard as marble to manage all that in twelve short hours, or else as coarse as mortar. She acts like it's a sacrifice, but deep down I know she enjoys it. Needs it, even. If it weren't for Wednesdays she couldn't be the mother she wants to be; she'd lose her mind. I watch her change diapers and fold the stroller into the trunk, and have the feeling that the person doing these things isn't her but someone else, someone moved by a sense of duty. The love she feels for Tinna is both loose and binding; she lives it as if it were prewritten and obeys it as if it were the stuff of legend. To me it's more like a parasite that has usurped her and now rides her in victory. I wonder where it is mothers go, once they stop following the rules. Samsa goes to Wednesdays. They are the public squares where she asserts her independence. She devours every Wednesday hour because every other hour of every other day is like a vampire that wants her with a love that bleeds her dry.

I don't get out of bed until I hear the sound of the car engine. Tinna is asleep in my arms. Samsa made sure to nurse her before leaving. I stroke her cheek and trace her veins, blue and green, with my fingertip. She is a life form so new it is still translucent—she still hasn't grown layers yet. She doesn't move or fuss. Nothing. Her neck is damp with sweat. I breathe in her scent, which smells of plants—of verbena and rue. I kiss her. She tastes medicinal. I loosen her pajamas a little, which are warm from all the warm things that she produces and consumes with her tiny milk-body. When she sleeps nuzzled against me like this, eyes flickering behind her eyelids, I feel as if life is facing up to me and saying the time has come for me to believe and let my guard down. When she wakes, I freshen her up, change her clothes, make her some baby food. She loves listening to the radio. She treats me to a performance that she never puts on in front of Samsa: she scoots around the kitchen on her butt, bumping along as she whistles like a kettle and glancing up at me, all laughter and drool. This is her way of asking for the radio to be turned on. Or at least I think it is, because the minute I do she gets down on all fours and scurries over to me. Then I take her in my arms, and we dance. I'm a terrible dancer; I have no sense of rhythm or any interest in moving my body in sync with another, except during sex. But a baby's willpower is one and whole, it knows exactly how to build everything up and tear it all down, how to make mountains and raze them to the ground. So I do something I never have with Samsa, I hold Tinna's body to me and explore the intimacy that wells up when the world closes around us. We dance. The music touches us with its fingertips, with its cold hands, as if it were removing our clothes. It catches us like a coastal flood carrying us further and further out. Holding Tinna like this makes me feel strange and new. It makes me think of all the words that have grown over me like hedges or weeds. Among them, one that's harder and older than any other in the world: *mother.*

. . .

I'm interested. I'd like to know her name, her occupation, where she lives. To walk through walls. I want to follow her home and head indoors in the dead of night, after smoking the anticipation. Inside, the furniture makes way for me in the half-dark. I have no trouble finding her. She's sleeping on a spotless bed set between two windows. Floating like she's on a lake. I step closer. There's so much naked skin, a fantastic pulp that radiates light, a migratory brilliance that spills across the room like sun through a woodland. It dawns on me that I could touch her. It dawns on me that if I kissed her, I would be stuck there. That the desire for a new woman is a fine line I walk, and it makes me anxious. I don't respond to it and instead beat a slow retreat, walk through the wall again, and head to the pub. Ragnar hugs me with a bottle still gripped in his hand, falls back on the bench and hears me out with his small, red eyes. He is an attentive, alcoholic creature, a friend. He doesn't laugh, he understands. I tell him about Samsa, about the woman with the pristine face and perfect bangs and malachite eyes, about sex—the fact that I'm not having any and how it calls to me. Resentment handpicks my words. I talk about women without counting myself among them. I'm not a woman. I am the cook on an old merchant ship, sharpening knives one edge at a time.

A morning in June. It's Wednesday and Tinna has been in the world for ten months, which is the same amount of time she spent marinating inside Samsa. We're going to cycle downtown to celebrate. She is thrilled about the idea of feeding bread to the ducks. I strap her into the baby seat, put on her helmet, take off her shoes and socks, and pedal as fast as I can. She loves the outdoors and is intoxicated by the speed. I lean over the handlebars. The sound of Tinna shrieking happily behind me cleaves the day in two. On one side, the pale and willful early-summer sun; on the other, the quiet docility of Wednesday mornings. The feel of Tinna's hands patting my lower back—that's all I need in life. Fifteen minutes later, we're at the pond. I park the bike and take the whole contraption apart. If I could access every minute I have dedicated to making sure Tinna is safe, I would squeeze them all into fifteen days and take her sailing with me. We would navigate the coast of Portugal and turn into the Mediterranean, into the waters of Africa or Italy, where the fish are small and blue, where their fat is sweet and melts like chocolate in the mouth.

Months without sex. The thing I find hardest to understand is Samsa's lightheartedness—her bright smile, the carefree kiss she plants on my lips every morning when she comes down for breakfast, radiating an incredible peace of mind, as if sleep had a magic touch. Whenever I try to hang onto her, she slinks off. I feel like an outlander who has chosen to honor her, out of ignorance, on the wrong date. We can't seem to stop and talk about it. We've put on weight in the space of our daily life, and now our seams are tearing stitch by stitch, exposing the shameful nakedness beneath.

I feel a permanent cold inside me, a whiff of extinction that has nothing to do with Iceland. It's the distance, the emptiness left when forces of the same inflow part ways. Unlike bears or goats, I had built my life on this emptiness, and lived it as though it were impossible to break. I have no future now, and no present either, outside of the foolish repetition of all the innocent chores that crop up day after day.

I spend mornings at museums trying to orchestrate a run-in with the curator. I can't find her. Hundreds of works of art hang on the walls and flow through each room like marble in a cemetery, with names and dates that are meaningless and do nothing to move me. I wish they made me feel something, at least once, that I could marvel at the light in a painting, at the blurred figures that awaken secret regions of the brain and send all the others to sleep. I'm not even interested in the sculptures—nude, still, deliberately feminine, wrested with every strike of the mallet from slabs of granite, from rocks that had once held meaning under the stars. I wander through the museums like a drifter down affluent avenues, the value of the pieces on show beyond my comprehension, their beauty out of my reach. They make me feel tiny, all told—whole but ordinary, so small and forgotten, lost to time, in a godforsaken place. I hate how clean things are on this island. I hate cleanliness that presumes perfection, I hate perfection worn like a smock over your Sunday best. My life with Samsa has turned into the same kind of façade, the day devoted to heaven, when no one goes to work and everyone smiles, the day when no one is allowed to touch. I don't believe in this island and I don't believe in happiness, or in relationships, or in children, or in God.

# 6

It's easier to put up a façade than it is to loosen the bolts you've been tightening, turn by turn, day by day, inside a house. I don't know why, though I suppose it could have something to do with casinos—with how easy it is to bet high on each new hand and how hard it is to walk away when you've run out of chips and begun to wonder whether you should play for your car, your watch, your daughter. I can't lay out a tablecloth and spray it with all the regret, resentment, and hunger I feel—a thick gruel of everything I've swallowed and haven't been able to keep down. When Samsa says goodnight and shuts the door to her bedroom, I think of how she's done this so many times it feels almost normal, of how we've inured the walls and conditioned the beds to our routine. Tinna waves goodbye with her tiny hand and laughs; I am no one to her now; this is the highlight of her day, the moment she gets to bury her tiny head between a pair of breasts and suckle them until she drifts off to sleep. I shut my door too, I shut my body away in a bed wedged within a short-term room inside a short-term house. In a city where, at night, in other beds, no one is saying goodnight or becoming inured or shutting themselves away.

• • •

Noon. She's back. Stunning in a sleek black dress and thick-framed glasses, in a pair of sandals that matches her purse and shows a single toe. She is an urban woman. She has domesticated every minor detail of her antelope body to fit the irresistible figure standing in front of me now. Her hair is geometric and still, so black it's almost blue, and frames a pair of vivid lips. I've never kissed lips with so much lipstick on them. Make-up usually turns me off, but I'd eat every last drop of hers. She orders a coffee and the word *coffee* travels along my chest like a drop of her sweat that trickles down my torso, skirts my belly button, and makes its fickle way to the smallest stitch of my body. I hand her the order, it'll be five hundred króna. She may not know who I am, but she knows what is happening, she knows I can glimpse her crouching in the weeds, that the wind has brought her to me—not just any wind but a slow and feverish breeze. A kid runs up to us, eyes the empanadas and leaves. She rummages through her purse. Her forearm, naked to the elbow, is briefly bathed in gold. I don't know why my mind jumps to places I've never been before, like Yemen and Somalia. To the very slender muscles under her dress. I picture them struggling beneath me, somewhere, anywhere, that same night.

As a safety measure, I get home early and cook up a storm. Lamb and potato stew with apricot meringue. Bread too. I work the dough in a large bowl. Flour and garlic powder, lukewarm water, salt, yeast. My muscles are ancient, the kind made to shape and knead. Muscles that control the bones—no one thinks for them, but they apply themselves, they get the job done, like the muscles that we love with. I stick the rolls in the oven and turn my attention to the lamb shoulder. I lay it out flat on the table. It's oily and dark like coffee. Raw, skinned meat doesn't look dead. It makes my mouth water, like certain kinds of perfume or Persian cucumbers. I cut with precision. My hands are knives, basting brushes, squeezers. I use them to manipulate food and also plunge them inside my head, where they braise the desire that occupies and perishes me. Desire cannot be killed, it can only be fermented and rocked to sleep. I cook to save myself. I cook ceaselessly. Tinna's laughter mixes like foam into peaks of sugar and egg whites. She plays hide-and-seek and shrieks with excitement when Samsa pretends that she can't find her and calls me over. Her voice trickles along the kitchen and living-room floors. I lap it up like a vinegar that can bleach me and break me up. Then I clean the stovetop and set the table, little by little, with no interest in sitting there.

She's gone for ten days and her absence doesn't so much soothe as upset me. It's much more rewarding to fight against myself than it is to struggle with facts and events. The outside world is a monster with as many heads as there are people that I love and fear. It doesn't care that I'm suffering; it snatches me up and gobbles me down, though not before chewing me to pieces first. The outside world is an acid-filled bathtub, an enormous stomach. The days dissolve into it, and

I live each one in the state of emergency that accompanies a storm; one second they've defeated me, the next I feel like I have them under control. The food truck has become an excuse, and I'm convinced I've lost my home. Not only my home but also the lamplights in every room, the words that twist and turn inside, and the bric-a-brac in the dresser. I feel displaced. But I'm human, so I push myself. I wait for this woman the way people wait for an earthquake to strike, or a drill—with panic, impatience, animal-like agitation: foul snouts to the ground, asses raised and open.

She shows up again one morning in July. White, sleeveless shirt, the nape of her neck exposed, skin perfectly tanned like a playgirl's. The moment she comes near me it clicks; she hadn't changed jobs or moved to a new neighborhood, she'd just gone on vacation to a place with sun, and its warmth and scent still cling to her body. I look at her and she smiles. I look at her and she walks straight up to me from the spot where she left her coat, her respectable life. We talk while I prepare the empanada. We talk as if with each word we were throwing together a pile of logs. The conversation takes us somewhere I've never been before, to the place where she swallowed me up for ten days and that I can't get out of my head. We make plans to meet for a pint that evening, late enough for one beer to turn into three or four and into a cocktail that will help us decide where we can go to forget ourselves. She drinks her coffee then and there. She lifts the cup to her mouth and blows on it with rounded, slender lips.

Her cheeks are sucked in. The froth on the coffee retreats with quiet reluctance to the edge of the cup. She drinks. A small sip that I slide into. I taste her lips before we've even kissed, and feel like an insect trapped in a flower. I have my fill of all the smells and textures and wander around absently with my wings tucked in. I ask for her name so that I can wear it as a keepsake as the day drags on as slow as ever. Anna, she says. And as she says this something runs aground, breaks open, floods with the force of water filling a void.

At home I shower and throw on some clean clothes. A pair of jeans and a T-shirt. I blow-dry my hair, which is something I only ever do in the winter. I comb it with my fingers and a bit of wax. I'm especially sensitive to the details that set this day apart from all the rest. Every gesture is a breadcrumb that I drop behind me. On its own, a single breadcrumb melts into the landscape. But many breadcrumbs together make up a trail. I think of mine as an avenue lined with streetlights and loudspeakers that sound off the news. I bury my dirty clothes in the laundry basket and brush my teeth twice. My intentions consume me, occupying me with the righteousness of a person reclaiming their ancestral land. I am acutely aware of their autonomy, to the point that I refuse to interfere—let them work things out among themselves. I hold my face in front of the mirror. I'm sure others do the same when they realize they're seeing their real face—that there is no mask. My skin is pale, delicate and easy to wrinkle, but looks young when untensed. I think of Anna, who can't be a day older than thirty and is all fist—the strength that shapes the hand and accentuates each bone. I scrub my nails with a brush. I think of her, and she unclothes. Her quiet body opens like a peony. I think of this, and don't know where to fall. I've done all I can to fight this thirst. The fact that I'm acting on this impulse doesn't make me guilty, it makes me human. I tell myself this and I believe it. I open the window, light a cigarette. I tell myself the same thing over again.

I can't believe Samsa doesn't suspect anything. But it seems like she has no idea. I wash the dishes after dinner and join them in the living room. Samsa bounces Tinna on her knees like she's a horse. Tinna laughs and throws her body back. She is fearless, defined by her confidence. I might have envied her had I not known the world would change her sooner or later. Life, which looks like a wide-open field, has already sprung holes. One day she'll grow up and feel stuck. Samsa notices I'm wearing shoes and wonders if I'm on my way out. Tinna claps her hands and asks for another go. She wants a wild horse, she wants to bounce at a gallop. Her passion is paralyzing. All that passion, in Samsa's handler arms, stirs up a chaos of emotion. Anger, anguish. And sadness, a sorrow that runs deep like the roots of a large tree that has just been logged. Sorrow holds me because it has tentacles; I am its sustenance, it stores me. I need to get out of here. All it takes is one night to flee the castle. All it takes is living there and being fine with the possibility of throwing yourself—like any other piece of rock—into the open sky.

We sit at a table by the window. Outside it's still bright. A residual, low-hanging light that grazes Anna's hair. We drink and chat and I get asked twice to put out my cigarette. She says she works as a stylist at a salon downtown. She loves her job. I think of all the museums I'd scoured for her and feel both stupid and unburdened, as if somehow my stupidity absolved me of the seriousness of my actions. I talk about my time working in the kitchen of a freighter, and my words unfurl a rich cloak that I'd like to wrap around her. She pores over every word with the thirst of a person who hasn't lived much. She holds me in her eyes, and I break their deep, green waters with strokes of my arms. I order another beer and she tells me about her trip to Capri. I couldn't care less. I don't listen, I stare. I picture her surrounded by pillows, laid out at a banquet. The skin of her forearms is smooth and clean, the skin of her thighs restless and overwarm. I could eat her with the calm deliberation of a person eating a bunch of grapes.

The yellow house waits at the end of the street. It looks tired under the streetlight, like it hasn't slept a wink. It recognizes me the moment we lock eyes, and indicts me with every last one of its windows. I realize the house is no longer a house but a wife that has grown over Samsa like a second skin that insulates and shelters her. A fresh layer of skin that wants for nothing and refuses to be touched, that wallpapers a generic name over the proper name of the woman I loved. I walk off the path and sit on the swings. Samsa bought the set less than two weeks ago and I've already made a habit of swinging there with Tinna every afternoon. To me the swing set may as well be a cage with a lion inside, its presence is as magnetic as it is horrifying. At the same time, I know now that it's impossible not to smile when pushing your kid on a swing. I tried, it can't be done. Small children have the power to impose their happiness on the everyday anxieties of grown-ups. Their power is short-lived, a gold dust that dresses the shoulders and reminds you that you're more than just an ordinary soldier, a sailor. It's hardly noticeable. Grown-ups have lost all interest in shiny things. A grown-up is the opposite of a magpie. Every morning when I make breakfast, the quiet, damp swing where I sit now resembles a witness to a minor crime.

Yesterday Samsa said the words *the strength of family ties.* She was on the phone in the entryway, and I was mopping the hall with the window cracked open when I'm sure I heard her say *the strength of family ties.* I kept rolling the bucket down the hall, to drown out the conversation and break away from the clause that gave shape to a dreadful thought. But *the strength of family ties* had already entered the house, like a curse with the power to overthrow all our certainties. Later that night, under the duvet, I was still shivering. I tried to think of the good things that bring people together. Generosity, gratitude, love. Maybe even respect and forgiveness. The brain makes it possible to do this—to pick out life-saving words, to set out new verdicts. It's the tool we kid ourselves with, as the body screams. I haven't slept properly in weeks. Sleep touches down, hits me, goes away. Touches down, hits me, goes away. Night in night out. Like a hyena that gnaws on me and leaves my bones exposed to the cold morning light. I think of *the strength of family ties* and I feel pain, my resident burrower. Limping along, using its crutch to stir up the fluids that cushion my knees. I've started taking sedatives with my morning coffee, and they make me feel distant. Sedatives turn you outward while alcohol turns you inward. Neither has anything to do with life, but with a numbness that makes living more bearable. Anna and I fuck once a week, which distances me from nothing and no one.

It takes three months to exhaust all interest in a body. I leave Anna the way I picked her up, without stopping to wonder if there might be a real person inside. I don't argue, I don't say goodbye. I leave her in the unhealthiest way there is. I vanish. Then comes the pursuit, which isn't so much a proper hunt as it is a way of drowning out the pain. She calls and leaves messages, and once she gets tired of doing that, she shows up at the food truck. I don't know why I didn't see it coming. I feel sunken, my brain dead inside me like the pointless treasure at the bottom of a fish tank. I work without thinking, as if I've been replaced with an earlier version of myself that is also well behaved. I go home early, I can't even bring myself to visit Ragnar. I notice Samsa has stopped touching me. I know because whenever Tinna does, I am returned to my body so quickly that it burns. I can barely think, I am strung along by decisions made a long time ago. I look forward to Wednesdays the way people look forward to spring, skin chapped and muscles withered. They are the warmth that the entire week watches over. Wednesdays roll in, and with them the feeling that I am teeming with leaves and larvae. I wander the city with Tinna strapped into her bike seat. We swim in pools and eat at cafés where she plays with other kids and laughs until she begins to rage with exhaustion. Then, I order a long black and sit her on my lap. She rests her tiny head against my chest and falls asleep in my arms, like a mussel clasped to a large rock. I watch people, slowly drinking my coffee as I draw out the journey to the sweetest, most merciful place imaginable.

She's come to the food truck three times. The first time, she was tentative. The second, furious. But Anna is a smart woman and the third time she seems refreshed, settled-down. Her purse spills over with contempt, every night we slept together sprayed against the wall, clawed free of every memory. I want her more than ever. She asks for the usual empanada and coffee, but doesn't touch the order or the money on the counter. She leaves the same way I left her, empty-handed, without saying goodbye. She rejects even the things I offer her in return for money, setting herself free.

As she walks away, I stare at her still-tanned legs and at the firm, round ass I'd held open so many times, softening and stoking every nerve, as well as the paper-thin membrane of skin that covers the hiddenmost regions of our bodies. She vanishes and I am left feeling that she has given me just the thing I needed, a slap in the face that will wake me up. I get back to work. I am much more focused now, present.

I've decided to salvage things. A strange feeling compels me, something like an impulse, a just-activated code, an organic, electrical thing that drives me forward with no need for my input. I form exaggerated thoughts that follow and time-stamp every action. The alternative would be to leave. I prepare the dough for tomorrow's empanadas. I give it a good knead, instilling it with the weightless life that the yeast will exhale overnight. Samsa's milk behaves this way too; it aerates Tinna and sends her to sleep just like the mass of dough I'm working on now, which has its own, unpredictable character, like every mass under the sun, or like clouds and waves and the stacks and stacks of years we hoard in our memories. I lower the shutters, empty the cash register, turn off the lights, and close up. The sky, low down as ever, is a large yawn. I bundle up and unlock my bike. I know what I'll do. I cycle to the grocery store, park, go inside. I don't like my life. I don't like the life of a person who goes out of their way to buy flowers. I tuck the flowers in the saddlebag and make my way home. It's Friday. Pub night. The night I had until recently spent with Anna.

I used to get home first thing Saturday morning. Donuts, croissants, the paper. I'd make some tea and orange juice, then have breakfast with Samsa, who'd heard me walk in and padded sleepily downstairs. She never asked questions, she couldn't stand Ragnar. There are some lives we don't like but are nonetheless mostly harmless, like the chlorine in our drinking water.

There are no lights on in the kitchen. None in the dining room, or in the living room either. But there is a faint glow in the window of the bedroom that for the moment belongs to Tinna and Samsa and will belong to me too after tonight. The time on my cell phone reads quarter to eight. They've turned in early, it's Friday and they're tired. I wish I could've made a different entrance. As I daydreamed about the house on my way there, I'd pictured it as a mansion like the ones in New Orleans or Savannah, all bright lights and splendor. I'd conjured a garden of unusual trees with subtropical trunks and branches on which lean pink wetland birds were sound asleep. I'd walked up the wide steps. I'd imagined the sort of life suited to a house made for galas and leisure. I'd heard its music. Then, I'd watched as I walked inside and held out a bouquet that would help me carve out a space for myself in the shared happiness of other people. I'd seen Samsa look at me, laughing the way she used to laugh before cordiality blunted the last of our intelligence and our passion. I'd seen Tinna struggle to her feet. I'd seen her rush toward me and hug my knees before she teetered and fell. As I made my way home, I'd laid out this entire future of hard work and resignation. A future just within reach.

It's sweltering inside. I take off my coat and sweater. Also, my jeans and shoes. I try not to make noise as I put together a tray with two glasses and a bottle of brennivín. Also, the flowers and massage oil. I carry everything upstairs. The bedroom door is closed, framed in a thin sliver of orange light. I leave the tray on the ground, listen carefully, hear nothing. I want Tinna to be asleep and for Samsa to still be awake. I turn the knob and crack open the door. I hope Tinna doesn't see me if she's still nursing, or else she'll get excited and we'll have a hard time putting her down. She's asleep. Tinna's asleep. But there's another baby in the room. Nipple in its mouth, eyes shut as it suckles, utterly intoxicated. Suckling and swallowing. Suckling and swallowing. White liquid dribbles down the baby's chin and vanishes into the folds of its neck. A disgusting dribble of milky drool. The nipple isn't Samsa's because Samsa is on her knees with her face buried between a pair of legs. Suckling and swallowing. Suckling and swallowing. Her breasts dangle over a pillow. The pillow is there to provide the perfect angle for the yawning cunt that Samsa is now eating out. Her breasts dangle and lurch. Tinna is digesting their contents, which curdle in the acid of her tiny stomach. The heat is unbearable. All the heat in the house has gathered into a cloud that smothers me. The nursing baby has a lot of work to do. Its mother moans quietly and tries not to writhe, but still writhes. Her enormous breasts rest on her ribs. She cradles the baby's head with her arm so that it won't unlatch. Samsa holds her legs at an angle, one in each hand, as the woman tilts her pelvis and pants. She's about to come. She presses the baby into her breast a little harder and has a steady, drawn-out orgasm, shuddering three or four times. I quietly shut the door. I'm weak, I feel sick. An awful fire burns under my skin, like a virulent case of scabies.

Saturday morning, I have breakfast with Samsa. Tea, orange juice, marmalade brioche. She says Tinna slept through the night, but that she had to take some valerian. She'd done a load of laundry while waiting for the effect to kick in. I smile and promise to take Tinna to feed the ducks so that she can get some shut-eye. Cordiality. The root of the word *cordiality* is an organ. An organ that pumps blood.

# 7

My cabinmate says Greenland is like a woman: born to wait. It's a miracle I don't slap her. Maybe the fact that she's my employer held me back. She sleeps on the top bunk, and finds it a bit harder every day to get up there. Her ass is fat and lumpy, as though instead of flesh it were filled with root vegetables, and her wristless arms come to an abrupt end at dark, stubby fingers that are impressively nimble. She's Colombian and I owe my job to her nationality—the interview took place in Spanish. I think she was looking forward to having someone to chat with in the evenings. No luck there. It's not that I think small talk is dumb, it's that I'm pretty sure it's more reckless than adopting a pet rat during a plague. But Emilia is a practical woman and she's hit on a solution that works for both of us. Convinced she likes poetry, she reads me a poem every night in a prayer-like drone. Neruda, Paz, Jodorowsky. She recites poetry and spouts obscenities. The thought of all the words that are implanted in us when we are young horrifies me. Now I know even poetry can't neutralize them, much less subdue them. I think of Tinna and feel unsteady. I think of Samsa and feel nothing, except the urge to get involved in something that's no longer mine.

I am driven by someone who isn't me. Someone who is no more than a voice.

Every ten days we sail from Reykjavík to Scoresby Sound, the largest fjord in the world. Time and again. Back and forth. Back and forth. If it weren't for the view, which slows down time and fills it with meaning whenever I take a smoke break, it'd be like taking the tram. This isn't a freighter, or a trawler. It's a cruise ship. Batches of passengers are conveyed inside, disperse, then leave. Someone counts them when they get on and counts them when they get off. The fact that they don't notice this is being done doesn't save them, because everything about them announces their end: their garish thermals, which are an affront to the leaden blue of the ocean, the land and the sky; the glut of food; the iPhones that frame their bodies and take their photographs. I wash dishes, mountains and mountains of white dishes with blue borders and the company logo. I know I won't ever be promoted, not even to assistant cook. I have a hunch this might be a symptom of Western decline: segregating the world of work from the world of experience, disqualifying bodies that have no credentials and tossing them out into the open sea. Without a title to vouch for my worth, I have no choice but to keep on cleaning plates with a high-pressure sprayer. Programming cleaning cycles, scrubbing pots and pans, unloading and organizing rounds of clean plates that exit the dishwasher in a cloud of steam, hot and shiny as if they'd just come from the earth's core. The salary is nothing compared to that of a ship's cook, though considerably more than what I'd make at the same job in Reykjavík. In any case, my expenses are minimal—just rent on a small apartment and child support for Tinna. I moved out after a month. The ground had lurched, opening cracks that then grew into gaping holes. Left on their own, the walls bled. I smoked during the day and drank with Ragnar at night. Samsa was the same person she had always been, but quieter. Her face lit up with Tinna and clouded over when she looked at me. She kissed me lightly, with caution. I felt like a traitor, like I was somehow responsible. It wasn't hard to find someone to take over the food truck. Ragnar started prying the booze out of my hands. I didn't fight back. I leaned into him and stared at the ceiling as it spun. I fell into the voices and laughter of the people around, and they caught me. It was a place at once dingy and well lit. It took me forever to light a cigarette. And I didn't smoke it. The ash fell on my chest. Sometimes a small burning ember.

The crew mess looks out onto the deck on the starboard side, the most popular. On my afternoon breaks I sit at the window and drink beer as I watch the passengers saunter by. It feels good not to be out there, with them. It feels good to be wearing a uniform, which makes me invisible. I stretch out my legs and bring the can to my lips. I have a sip. The beer fizzes in my mouth and loosens me up. It distracts from the exhaustion, which grows small and makes room for my thoughts. I realize I have memories, always the same ones. In them are Tinna and Samsa. Some are so old that they've been around the world. They're dug into my skin like fishhooks. I don't know what to do about them, whether to watch as they waste away or wait for them to leave on their own. I down the beer. The passengers annoy me. A frosted, double-glazed window separates us. I am part of another world, of an inhospitable land. It's pleasant here. Everyone outside has company and is wearing too many layers. All I can see are ruddy faces, mouths that laugh and let out clouds of breath. I'd find it impossible to do what they're doing. I can't live every day chasing after that kind of life. A life with no fat, meant for consumption only. When I undress in the evening, the turtleneck snags at my head and reminds me that birth is nothing at all—the danger lies in being reborn.

I get Tinna for four or five days a month, and that's all I need. Really, it's plenty. I don't feel the need to be a mother to her, at least not the kind Samsa thinks I should be. I'm not interested in the web of daily obligations that ensnares Tinna, all I want is to spend time with her, to be with her. Which is perfectly fine by Samsa. My decision has underscored the importance of her cause. I look at her and see a woman who has sacrificed her own self-worth for the well-being of a child. The queen of good decision-making, she has everything under control. Tinna is her clay, her figurine, so small she can fit in the palm of her hand. A mother's life can be this: a tongue that never tires of licking. Samsa is useful, is loving, is practical. She has become a lodestar. Tinna cherishes her with the kind of love that is bolstered by day after day lived under the same roof. She's chosen her, and this makes me feel better. Like she's saving me. I often think of leaving, I will it every time we sail past a fishing boat. I could say goodbye to the dishwashing gig and instead process mountains of fish. Month after grueling month at high sea. Long days of work. Dealing with living things, even if it means gutting them and ending up spattered in entrails. I don't know why the thought of a dead cod soothes my pain. And I don't understand the pain, which is a minor but ever-present discomfort. I assumed it would take advantage of the fact that I was exhausted to sink its claws and teeth into my flesh. I was ready to cry. Instead, the pain is doglike. It sits in a corner, licking my wound. Making sure it stays open and tender. I sail and I am all alone. Tomorrow we dock, and I will go fetch Tinna. I won't be boarding any other boats, at least for now.

Dear readers,

As well as relying on bookshop sales, And Other Stories relies on subscriptions from people like you for many of our books, whose stories other publishers often consider too risky to take on.

Our subscribers don't just make the books physically happen. They also help us approach booksellers, because we can demonstrate that our books already have readers and fans. And they give us the security to publish in line with our values, which are collaborative, imaginative and 'shamelessly literary'.

All of our subscribers:

- receive a first-edition copy of each of the books they subscribe to
- are thanked by name at the end of our subscriber-supported books
- receive little extras from us by way of thank you, for example: postcards created by our authors

## BECOME A SUBSCRIBER, OR GIVE A SUBSCRIPTION TO A FRIEND

Visit andotherstories.org/subscriptions to help make our books happen. You can subscribe to books we're in the process of making. To purchase books we have already published, we urge you to support your local or favourite bookshop and order directly from them – the often unsung heroes of publishing.

## OTHER WAYS TO GET INVOLVED

If you'd like to know about upcoming events and reading groups (our foreign-language reading groups help us choose books to publish, for example) you can:

- join our mailing list at: andotherstories.org
- follow us on Twitter: @andothertweets
- join us on Facebook: facebook.com/AndOtherStoriesBooks
- admire our books on Instagram: @andotherpics
- follow our blog: andotherstories.org/ampersand

# CURRENT & UPCOMING BOOKS

01 Juan Pablo Villalobos, *Down the Rabbit Hole*, trans. Rosalind Harvey

02 Clemens Meyer, *All the Lights*, trans. Katy Derbyshire

03 Deborah Levy, *Swimming Home*

04 Iosi Havilio, *Open Door*, trans. Beth Fowler

05 Oleg Zaionchkovsky, *Happiness is Possible*, trans. Andrew Bromfield

06 Carlos Gamerro, *The Islands*, trans. Ian Barnett

07 Christoph Simon, *Zbinden's Progress*, trans. Donal McLaughlin

08 Helen DeWitt, *Lightning Rods*

09 Deborah Levy, *Black Vodka: ten stories*

10 Oleg Pavlov, *Captain of the Steppe*, trans. Ian Appleby

11 Rodrigo de Souza Leão, *All Dogs are Blue*, trans. Zoë Perry and Stefan Tobler

12 Juan Pablo Villalobos, *Quesadillas*, trans. Rosalind Harvey

13 Iosi Havilio, *Paradises*, trans. Beth Fowler

14 Ivan Vladislavić, *Double Negative*

15 Benjamin Lytal, *A Map of Tulsa*

16 Ivan Vladislavić, *The Restless Supermarket*

17 Elvira Dones, *Sworn Virgin*, trans. Clarissa Botsford

18 Oleg Pavlov, *The Matiushin Case*, trans. Andrew Bromfield

19 Paulo Scott, *Nowhere People*, trans. Daniel Hahn

20 Deborah Levy, *An Amorous Discourse in the Suburbs of Hell*

21 Juan Tomás Ávila Laurel, *By Night the Mountain Burns*, trans. Jethro Soutar

22 SJ Naudé, *The Alphabet of Birds*, trans. the author

23 Niyati Keni, *Esperanza Street*

24 Yuri Herrera, *Signs Preceding the End of the World*, trans. Lisa Dillman

25 Carlos Gamerro, *The Adventure of the Busts of Eva Perón*, trans. Ian Barnett

26 Anne Cuneo, *Tregian's Ground*, trans. Roland Glasser and Louise Rogers Lalaurie

27 Angela Readman, *Don't Try This at Home*

28 Ivan Vladislavić, *101 Detectives*

29 Oleg Pavlov, *Requiem for a Soldier*, trans. Anna Gunin

30 Haroldo Conti, *Southeaster*, trans. Jon Lindsay Miles

31 Ivan Vladislavić, *The Folly*

32 Susana Moreira Marques, *Now and at the Hour of Our Death*, trans. Julia Sanches

33 Lina Wolff, *Bret Easton Ellis and the Other Dogs*, trans. Frank Perry

34 Anakana Schofield, *Martin John*

35 Joanna Walsh, *Vertigo*

36 Wolfgang Bauer, *Crossing the Sea*, trans. Sarah Pybus with photographs by Stanislav Krupař

37 Various, *Lunatics, Lovers and Poets: Twelve Stories after Cervantes and Shakespeare*

38 Yuri Herrera, *The Transmigration of Bodies*, trans. Lisa Dillman

39 César Aira, *The Seamstress and the Wind*, trans. Rosalie Knecht

40 Juan Pablo Villalobos, *I'll Sell You a Dog*, trans. Rosalind Harvey

41 Enrique Vila-Matas, *Vampire in Love*, trans. Margaret Jull Costa

42 Emmanuelle Pagano, *Trysting*, trans. Jennifer Higgins and Sophie Lewis

43 Arno Geiger, *The Old King in His Exile*, trans. Stefan Tobler

44 Michelle Tea, *Black Wave*

45 César Aira, *The Little Buddhist Monk*, trans. Nick Caistor

46 César Aira, *The Proof*, trans. Nick Caistor

47 Patty Yumi Cottrell, *Sorry to Disrupt the Peace*

48 Yuri Herrera, *Kingdom Cons*, trans. Lisa Dillman

49 Fleur Jaeggy, *I am the Brother of XX*, trans. Gini Alhadeff

50 Iosi Havilio, *Petite Fleur*, trans. Lorna Scott Fox

51 Juan Tomás Ávila Laurel, *The Gurugu Pledge*, trans. Jethro Soutar

52 Joanna Walsh, *Worlds from the Word's End*

53 Nicola Pugliese, *Malacqua*, trans. Shaun Whiteside

54 César Aira, *The Lime Tree*, trans. Chris Andrews

55 Ann Quin, *The Unmapped Country*

56 Fleur Jaeggy, *Sweet Days of Discipline*, trans. Tim Parks

57 Alicia Kopf, *Brother in Ice*, trans. Mara Faye Lethem

58 Christine Schutt, *Pure Hollywood*

59 Cristina Rivera Garza, *The Iliac Crest*, trans. Sarah Booker

60 Norah Lange, *People in the Room*, trans. Charlotte Whittle

61 Kathy Page, *Dear Evelyn*

62 Alia Trabucco Zerán, *The Remainder*, trans. Sophie Hughes

63 Amy Arnold, *Slip of a Fish*

64 Rita Indiana, *Tentacle*, trans. Achy Obejas

65 Angela Readman, *Something Like Breathing*

66 Gerald Murnane, *Border Districts*

67 Gerald Murnane, *Tamarisk Row*

68 César Aira, *Birthday*, trans. Chris Andrews

69 Ann Quin, *Berg*

70 Fleur Jaeggy, *Proleterka*, trans. Alastair McEwen

71 Olivia Rosenthal, *To Leave with the Reindeer*, trans. Sophie Lewis

72 Lina Wolff, *The Polyglot Lovers*, trans. Saskia Vogel

73 Mario Levrero, *Empty Words*, trans. Annie McDermott

74 Michelle Tea, *Against Memoir*

75 Cristina Rivera Garza, *The Taiga Syndrome*, trans. Suzanne Jill Levine and Aviva Kana

76 Hanne Ørstavik, *Love*, trans. Martin Aitken

77 Tim Etchells, *Endland*

78 Rita Indiana, *Made in Saturn*, trans. Sydney Hutchinson

79 Luke Brown, *Theft*

80 Gerald Murnane, *Collected Short Fiction*

81 Gerald Murnane, *Invisible Yet Enduring Lilacs*

82 James Attlee, *Isolarion*

83 Deb Olin Unferth, *Barn 8*

84 Juan Pablo Villalobos, *I Don't Expect Anyone to Believe Me*, trans. Daniel Hahn

85 Andrzej Tichý, *Wretchedness*, trans. Nichola Smalley

86 Yuri Herrera, *A Silent Fury: The El Bordo Mine Fire*, trans. Lisa Dillman

87 Lina Wolff, *Many People Die Like You*, trans. Saskia Vogel

88 Ann Quin, *Three*

89 Rachel Genn, *What You Could Have Won*

90 John Metcalf, *Medals and Prizes*

91 Claudia Hernández, *Slash and Burn*, trans. Julia Sanches

92 Ann Quin, *Passages*

93 Various, *This Is How We Come Back Stronger*

94 Eva Baltasar, *Permafrost*, trans. Julia Sanches

95 Norah Lange, *Notes from Childhood*, trans. Charlotte Whittle

96 James Attlee, *Under the Rainbow: Voices from the First Lockdown*

97 César Aira, *The Divorce*, trans. Chris Andrews

98 Mario Levrero, *The Luminous Novel*, trans. Annie McDermott

99 Tice Cin, *Keeping the House*

100 Yuri Herrera, *Three Novels*, trans. Lisa Dillman

101 Elisa Victoria, *Oldladyvoice*, trans. Charlotte Whittle

102 Sammy Wright, *Fit*

103 Robin McLean, *Pity the Beast*

104 Mona Arshi, *Somebody Loves You*

105 Paulo Scott, *Phenotypes*, trans. Daniel Hahn

106 Robert Aickman, *Go Back at Once*

107 Adrian Nathan West, *My Father's Diet*

108 Alia Trabucco Zerán, *When Women Kill: Four Crimes Retold*, trans. Sophie Hughes

109 Preti Taneja, *Aftermath*

110 Barry Hines, *The Gamekeeper*

111 Gerald Murnane, *Last Letter to a Reader*

112 Fleur Jaeggy, *The Water Statues*, trans. Gini Alhadeff

113 Najwa Barakat, *Mister N*, trans. Luke Leafgren

114 Jessi Jezewska Stevens, *The Visitors*

115 James Greer, *Bad Eminence*

116 Juan Pablo Villalobos, *Invasion of the Spirit People*, trans. Rosalind Harvey

117 Eva Baltasar, *Boulder*, trans. Julia Sanches

118 Ann Quin, *Tripticks*

Eva Baltasar has published ten volumes of poetry to widespread acclaim. Her debut novel, *Permafrost*, received the 2018 Premi Llibreter from Catalan booksellers and was shortlisted for France's 2020 Prix Médicis for Best Foreign Book. It is the first novel in a triptych that aims to explore the universes of three different women in the first person. The author lives a simple life with her wife and two daughters in a village near the mountains.

Julia Sanches translates from Portuguese, Spanish, and Catalan. For And Other Stories she has translated from all three languages—from the Portuguese, *Now and at the Hour of Our Death* by Susana Moreira Marques; from the Catalan, *Permafrost* by Eva Baltasar; and from the Spanish, *Slash and Burn* by Claudia Hernández, for which she won a PEN/Heim award. Born in São Paulo, Brazil, Julia currently lives in Providence, Rhode Island.